FORGOTTEN GHOSTS

To all those weighed down by the tattered baggage of their past,
it's gonna be okay. You can do this.

FORGOTTEN GHOSTS

CASS KAY

Defiant Dandelions Publishing

I

Stalkers and Coffee

Vianna was being watched. Stalked, actually. The hairs on her arms raised, dimpling her skin. The reaction from her body wasn't an exact science that definitively proved anything, but as she shoved the tip of her garden spade into the cold soil, she knew.

Crouching there, on her hands and knees in an upturned flower bed, she pretended everything was normal, that she was none the wiser. But only half of her attention was on the ground; the other half was on the movement in her peripheral vision. She'd worked herself into a damp sweat despite the crisp autumn air, and her long-sleeved shirt clung to her skin.

She sat back on her heels, grabbed a tulip bulb from the bag at her side, and plopped it into the first hole. Her stalker froze, hidden by the trees on the other side of the fence. Vianna's demon familiar, Shuck, rumbled in her chest. Being bonded to a demon was a new experience, and Vianna was still adjusting. He sent a wave of eagerness through her. He wanted to handle the threat, but she preferred methods that didn't involve a bloody, mutilated mess. Shuck had bonded with the last eleven generations of Roots witches, all of whom could reasonably be categorized as paid assassins. His methods for handling situations weren't something Vianna trusted.

With a scrunched nose, she kept her focus on the task, resisting the urge to look into the trees. She emptied the rest of the bag, bulb by bulb, into the row of holes she had prepared, scooped soil over each, then smashed in a cut section of chicken wire over the top. She spread a layer of compost, then sprinkled cayenne pepper as the last step.

Giving in to the urge, she glanced over her shoulder toward the trees. Black, beady eyes stared back. His bushy tail framed a plump, furry body. He *should* be plenty plump after the amount of bulbs he'd gorged on in the past few weeks. The squirrel—aka her stalker—had shown no discrimination in his pilferings; all flavors of bulbs were succulent treasures in his greedy paws. It was an all-out war, and Vianna was losing. Badly.

The hinges on the porch screen door squeaked as it swung open. "How long have you been out here?"

Vianna swiveled around. "I don't know. The sun was up." *Almost.*

Dee stood on the deck wearing a kimono covered with purple hibiscus and a matching hair wrap. She cupped a steaming mug, showcasing her matching manicure. The woman was a goddess with coffee—all drinks, really. In the past three months of living together, Vianna had learned not to question when Dee put a drink in her hand. Mother's gasoline-grade moonshine sat untouched in the pantry, along with Vianna's ability to hide away in a mason jar. She was working on herself: facing things instead of running, opening up in order to maintain *real* relationships. Luckily, Dee was patient. Mostly. They'd had a few moments.

"I can hear you rummaging through the house at all hours. It's mind-boggling that you don't think sleep is amazing." Dee stood at the edge of the porch.

Vianna gathered the leftover supplies from her war strategy. "I never said sleep isn't amazing. I would love to sleep as much as you do."

"Explain to me again why you don't?"

"I don't think insomnia is exactly explainable." The new nightmares of Mother burying Vianna alive weren't helping. But since her insomnia had plagued her long before this newest round of night terrors, she couldn't blame her restlessness on them. Plus, mentioning them to Dee would only start a full investigation into every nightmare Vianna had ever had, making her relive each one in vivid detail. She'd rather not. Not this early.

Dee turned with a flourish, her satin robe fluttering around her calves, and headed back into the house. Vianna stood and brushed away the dirt clumps that clung to the knees of her jeans. Her stalker had vanished, trying to lead her into a false sense of security. She hoped the cayenne pepper not only burned his tongue but got stuck in the crevices of his tiny little paws.

The smell of freshly brewed coffee lured Vianna inside. She took off her shoes at the door and moved to the sink, washing her hands with a worn bar of homemade lavender-lemon soap. On the counter sat her old chipped mug that wafted the faintest hint of cinnamon.

"That twattle-basket yowls louder than a coyote. Not every neighboring ear needs to be privy to your life." Grandma Susannah stood in the archway between the kitchen and living room. Vianna didn't even bother looking over her shoulder because some things never changed. Grandma would be wearing the same brown peasant dress, dirt-smudged apron, and thick rope noose around her neck like an oversized necklace. Ghosts didn't change their clothes.

Twattle-basket was one of the many names Grandma had used over the past few months in reference to Dee. Vianna wasn't entirely sure what they all meant, but she suspected they centered around someone who was loud or gossipy. Regardless, Dee's brand of loud was a relief for Vianna, replacing the weird creaks that filled the silence, and Vianna was grateful to have her as a roommate. She dried her hands on one of the dish towels with embroidered rainbows that Dee had ordered online, then scooped up her mug of liquid heaven.

"She should focus on her talents instead of waggling her tongue," Grandma huffed. "Put her on the cauldron."

Vianna grinned into her mug as she walked through Grandma, ignoring her. What Grandma really wanted was to learn the secrets of potion making. The art was finicky, and it was a rarity for someone to be as competent as Dee. Grandma clicked her tongue before fading from the room.

Dee sat in the living room, curled up in the same corner of the couch as always, closest to the fireplace. Black-and-white photos of witches past lined the mantel. They were among the few things that had survived Hurricane Dee in the Great Redecoration. There was no conversation about keeping or removing them; they just... belonged.

Dee nodded her chin toward a newspaper resting on the coffee table. "Check out the front page."

Every bit of news interested Dee: new species of bees, Sephora's latest seasonal color, the real estate rates in California, or any new rock formation containing evidence of evolution. Hailing from a long line of coven historians made information in all forms invaluable. Her thirst for knowledge was admirable, but sometimes overwhelming. Summaries were a good compromise. "It's cold," Vianna said, shuffling toward the fireplace. "I'll make a fire while you give me the CliffsNotes."

"Not this one." Dee scrunched her face. "It's not pleasant, but I don't want you learning about it elsewhere. Fire first. My toes are ice cubes." Starting fires was Dee's kryptonite. She tried but somehow only filled the house with smoke.

Vianna set her mug on the coffee table, then crouched by the hearth. Pine cones rubbed in nutmeg, cinnamon, and other fall spices were piled into a pyramid in the firebox—fire starters were one of her insomnia-induced hobbies. She pulled on her connection to Shuck, waiting for the deep rumble that would reverberate through her bones. A current of energy started from beneath the marking on her collarbone, spreading down her arm, then sparking like electricity at her fingertips.

She snapped her index finger against her thumb, and the wick in the center of the cones sparked with fire. Tendrils of smoke twirled into the air, filling the room with the scent of autumn spices.

The flames grew quickly, and waves of heat warmed the room. Vianna stood and headed toward the couch, checking for any remnants of gardening that still clung to her before flopping onto the middle cushion. Dee was not-so-patiently staring, nails tapping on her mug. Vianna grabbed the newspaper and rested against the back of the couch with a huff. The front page featured a photo of a couple standing on the steps of the Salem Essex Museum.

Vianna stared at the photo, speechless.

Charles Barton, the owner of the museum and sexual predator, stood next to Original Blood Coven member Tiphonie Parker. The headline read, "Essex Museum to Display Exhibit on Elizabeth Derby West".

She didn't bother reading the article; the picture was enough. She forced down the lump in her throat. Tiphonie was a rotten brat, but no one deserved Charles. Not to mention the battle between their mothers that had resulted in the death of Tiphonie's mother, and the institution of Charles's in the Danvers State Hospital.

Dee sighed. "We could dig a hole in the backyard. No one would miss him. Well, besides the coven purse strings."

Vianna tossed the paper into the fire, and it burst into a ball of blue light over the pinecones. An extra wave of heat pushed through the room.

"Hey, I hadn't finished reading that." Despite her outcry, Dee was already making swiping motions on her phone.

"His mother killed hers—right in front of her." Vianna glanced over her shoulder, toward the landing at the bottom of the stairs where it all had happened. The battle had sprouted from a missing page in the Roots family grimoire, a page that was still missing. That detail had been lost in the shuffle of funerals and coven politics, but Vianna hadn't forgotten.

"She can't be that clueless." Vianna would never understand legacy witches, much less Tiphonie.

"She's all about getting the vote for coven mother. The Barton name can provide liquid cash, and that's irresistible for a coven that has none." Dee pulled her feet underneath her and adjusted.

Vianna scoffed. "And I guess everyone just forgot the *obvious* detail that the Barton name is the entire reason why the coven is broke."

"And motherless," Dee added. "Plus, with Charles running for mayor, he's looking to make sure the coven still backs him now that *mother dearest* is in the psych ward."

"Don't remind me." The signs plastered throughout town with Charles's trademark dimples were enough to make Vianna gag. They'd briefly dated, three dates precisely, before she knocked him over the head with a shovel in self-defense. They hadn't spoken since.

The theme song from *Ghostbusters* rang from the kitchen.

"Refill me while you're up?" Dee held out her mug with a wide grin. She'd changed the ringtone on Vianna's phone, and they both knew it.

With a groan, Vianna pushed herself up, giving Dee a fake scowl and snagging her mug on the way to the kitchen. Her phone sat on the counter as it charged, and the screen lit with the name Tucker Etienne. He'd been gone all week for his sister's wedding to some big shot down in New Orleans.

She set down the mugs and picked up her phone. "Tuck?"

"Hey," he answered.

Vianna refilled the mugs with one hand and held the phone with the other. "Your sister get hitched yet?"

"Almost. Tonight's the night, not that you could tell. She's more focused on finding every single gay man within a hundred-mile radius to throw at me. Apparently, if she's getting married, her big brother needs to be heading down the aisle soon, too."

Vianna gave a snort at that. Tuck was work obsessed and didn't seem all that interested in dating or marriage from what she saw.

"You busy?" Tuck asked. "I've got a favor to ask."

"Maybe." She put the coffeepot back on the burner. "Let's hear it."

"I need someone to check on Ashley."

"Ashley?" Vianna asked. "Why?"

Ashley worked at Tuck's shop, Sticks and Bones. Although he owned the shop, she ran the front for tourists while he ran the back, where the real hoodoo happened. Vianna suspected the front shop paid for the back and was the entire reason Tuck bothered with tourists. In the past three months since moving back to Salem, she'd had weekly lunches with Tuck, and she couldn't count how many times she'd waited while he helped some community member or another. She'd yet to see him charge even so much as a dime for any of it.

"I had a few clients ping me about weird things around the shop. I called Ashley, but she's pretending like everything is normal." He hesitated. "She sounded strange. Something is up."

"What kind of *weird* things are people seeing?"

There was a long pause on the other end. Vianna rested her hip against the counter as she waited.

"Unfamiliar spirits," Tuck said. That explained the hesitancy. He knew Vianna saw ghosts, and he also knew how much she hated it. "If it was just that, I'd wait until I got home tomorrow evening. But they also mentioned a surge of power in the aura around the shop. And maybe a feeling of ill intent. Something is up, and Denise will kill me if I miss her vows."

"Very true." Vianna knew his sister, and she actually might kill him if he missed her wedding. She was big on family.

Dee walked into the kitchen and took over with the coffee, adding in cream and using the cinnamon shaker. She tilted her head with raised brows in Vianna's direction.

"What exactly do you want me to do?" Vianna asked Tuck. Even if the shop did have a ghost problem, she wasn't sure what she could do about it. Seeing ghosts was not the same as exorcising them. She'd been able to banish ghosts from her property only because she'd had something from their physical body: a decaying hand for Nancy, the blood on a pair of scissors for the bathroom haunt, and her own blood had worked on her uncle in the upstairs bedroom.

"You don't have to do anything. Just swing by, then tell me what you see. I need someone to be my eyes so I know how serious this is. I'll handle the rest."

"Fine." Vianna sighed. "I'll stop by."

"I owe you."

"Yeah, yeah. Talk soon." Vianna hung up.

"Our very first case." Dee nudged a mug toward Vianna.

"Nope."

"That's not what you told Tuck."

Vianna scrunched her nose at Dee as she stretched out her sore neck muscles from working in the garden.

The corners of Dee's lips twitched. "Where we going?"

It was easiest not to argue with her. "Tuck's shop. He thinks Ashley might have a ghost problem she's not fessing up to."

"Ghosts?" Dee squealed. "That's perfect for our first official paranormal investigation!"

"No," Vianna said. "Absolutely not. We're just swinging by to take a peek, then letting Tuck know what we see. No investigation required."

"We're going to need a good name. Give me at least forty minutes to get ready. Don't leave without me." Dee narrowed her eyes at Vianna for emphasis before heading upstairs. "We better make it snappy, though. I've still got some prep to do for the market tonight, and you *are* coming."

The witch market was an annual free-for-all trade and barter for witches, cloaked with magic to keep humans unaware. Vianna was more than a little tempted to go. She could thin out the candle den from her overstock and make a few bucks in the process. But she'd need a booth to do that, and solitary witches couldn't get booths. They were dispersed to covens only.

"I'm not going to the market just so every Salem witch can glare at me," Vianna mumbled under her breath. She stalked back into the living room and stood by the fire. "And I'm only taking a quick peek at Tuck's shop to see what kind of ghosts we're dealing with," she said out loud to no one.

There would be no witch market and no official paranormal investigation.

2

Red, White, and Blue

Sticks and Bones, Tuck's store, was located smack in the middle of downtown on Essex Street. And to get there, they had to battle the thick crowds. The living bustled in clusters among the dead, which only Vianna could see. In every direction there were death loops, like walking through a town of macabre performers at a Shakespearean festival. There were both pistol and sword duels, carriage and car accidents, and, of course, bloodied fists and blades.

She kept her focus downward. The view of her brown leather boots mucking through the golden leaves was far better than the death all around her. She squeezed through clusters of witches and non-witches alike with Dee right behind her, and it wasn't until they were a few feet from a raised stage that realization dawned. The crowd wasn't because of the tourist season. She stopped dead in her tracks.

In the center of a circular plaza was a stage where Tiphonie and the Ramsey twins stood. The trio gathered to the right of a podium, the twins in pressed, white business suits and Tiphonie in a red skirt suit. Behind them, tall banners read Mayor Barton in bold, patriotic colors. Local shops formed a backdrop: a tavern advertising fresh fish and chips, a crystal boutique, and a witchy home decor store.

Tiphonie smoothed her up-twist hairdo despite not having a single red hair out of place. When her eyes locked with Vianna's, her shoulders slumped for a fraction of a moment, but then she lifted her chin and jerked her head away. The Ramsey twins, instead, doubled down with their glares. The one on the right flicked her thick, blond braid from her shoulder, and the other used two fingers to double-point at Vianna. Movement shifted from the sides of the stage in response.

A huddle of older witches in scratchy-looking couch-fabric suits stepped from behind a banner. Their narrowed eyes followed the hand gesture from the Ramsey twin, focusing them on Vianna. Witch security. Looked like Charles was already backed in his political campaign by the Original Blood Coven. They must be confident that the Bartons would funnel funds back into the coven if they provided security and arm candy.

Charles took to the podium in a black suit and red tie, his hair slicked to the side. He gave a large pearly smile, complete with dimples, and the crowd roared with applause. It was just her luck to stumble upon one of his campaign speeches.

"Ladies and gentlemen of Salem, new and familiar faces, I'm honored by your show of support." Charles's voice boomed from the speakers.

Memories suddenly flooded back: her head clogged with a magically induced fog, his hands slipping beneath her clothes, and his hot breath on her neck. She felt nauseous but planted her hands on her hips, refusing to hug herself and shrink into her sweater. She might feel sick, but she would stand tall.

He continued. "Looking out into the crowd, into all these faces

I've known my whole life, I see myself. There's a part of each of you in my upbringing."

As if what he'd said was some deeply profound realization, he took a long pause before continuing. "No one knows the real Salem like I do. And I'm here to tell you that each and everyone of you matters. Your voice is heard, and your face is seen—by me. It doesn't matter what your last name is or what side of the tracks you come from. I'm here to promise you that all of Salem's residents will be heard if I'm elected mayor."

More applause erupted, and Vianna wanted to hurl her breakfast. The only thing Charles cared about was how to use people to his advantage. His promises to unite, help, or whatever he was trying to say were as hollow as a termite-infested trunk. Dee groaned, drawing a glare from a pair of supporters in red Barton for Mayor t-shirts.

As Charles continued on about some new Salem for all, the witch security team broke through the crowd with Mistress Zosia Ramsey in the lead. She was unmistakable with her towering height and jutting chin. Just like her twin daughters, she had glossy blonde hair, but hers was cut in a sharp bob that was longer in the front.

"It's disappointing to see you here, Vianna." Zosia didn't look away, didn't fiddle with her pearl-trimmed suit, but stood still as granite, watching. It was disconcerting.

Vianna folded her arms. "At least I'm consistent."

"Hmm," said Zosia, "I won't allow any trouble today—from you or anyone else."

"*You're* in charge?" Dee stood beside Vianna.

Zosia grinned, but not the welcoming kind, the type of smile a predator gave before eating its prey. And she kept her attention on Vianna with not so much as a glance spared toward Dee. The snatch wasn't going to answer her. Zosia and her posse crowded Vianna and Dee, nudging them away from the crowd and creating a speck of privacy.

It was pointless to say anything, much less ask questions. They should just walk away. Instead, Vianna blurted the words burning like acid on her lips. "How can the coven support *that*?" She flicked a hand in Charles's direction.

Zosia raised a brow and gave a slight chuckle. "The coven doesn't *support* non-coven members. They control them. Rose owes the coven, which means what was hers is now ours. I realize you're a solitary, and as such, some things are beyond your understanding, but really, Vianna, you were raised properly despite your spectacular failure as a witch. You know these things."

Of course it was all about the money, and Vianna knew that. Charles wasn't some golden trophy, but part of a debt to be paid. His finances would be sucked dry, as the coven needed to repair the damage from his mother, and having political supporters donate money to his campaign gave them more to work with. Running for office may not have even been his idea. That still didn't answer why Tiphonie was stomaching him or what had happened to the missing page from the Roots grimoire. But Zosia wasn't going to give Vianna those answers, so Vianna didn't bother asking.

"There's no need for you here, dear. Go play elsewhere." Zosia raised her hand, shooing Vianna.

She didn't want to be there, but now she sure as hell wouldn't run along like some child. Zosia straightened, appearing somehow even taller, which seemed almost inhuman. Dee looped an arm with Vianna, squeezing her elbow in the classic don't-make-a-scene communication. It wasn't that Vianna tried to make dramatic scenes; it was that she seemed to stumble head first directly into them.

"Come on." Dee tugged Vianna away, down the cobbled sidewalk and away from the crowds.

Vianna looked over her shoulder at the stage, where Tiph and the Ramsey twins smiled, and Charles puffed his chest over some declaration of hard work that he knew nothing about. Zosia waved in an irritating ta-ta fashion. And the adoring crowd would never see them as Vianna saw them, because they would only ever see the public version: the staged image, rehearsed message, and fake smiles.

"They're not worth it," Dee said as they put more distance between them and the political crowds.

Logically, Dee was right. But Vianna's anger toward Charles wasn't appeased by the logical option. He shouldn't get to win, to take advantage of more people for his own gain. The thought tightened her gut into a rock, and more uninvited memories flashed before her of Charles's fingers dancing up her spine. She shuddered. Charles *did* have every advantage. And there wasn't a damn thing Vianna could do about it.

She nudged Dee to the edge of the sidewalk, veering around a ghost as he collapsed to his knees, a knife lodged in his gut with bulging eyes staring forward. Blood seeped through his cotton tunic. She walked faster, putting behind the frustrations of Charles and the coven.

They walked a few blocks in silence, and Vianna tried to calm herself. She breathed deeply and counted to five in her head. The moaning of Giles Corey played like a morbid soundtrack in the background. It'd taken her a few years to figure out who he was and why he made those noises. He'd been killed during the witch trials, in between the tourist shops and the impromptu political rally. Giles had been one of the only men accused and dealt with in Salem instead of being carted off to Boston. When he'd refused to plead neither guilty nor not guilty, community members stacked boulders on top of his chest in order to press the words from him. Instead, they'd pressed the life from him.

"You okay?" Dee asked softly.

"No," Vianna admitted as they passed the display window of the thrift store with their monster dolls. A new zombie had been added: a small boy with suspenders. She scrunched her nose at the large Barton campaign sign in the corner of the window.

"At least..." Dee went silent for a moment, making Vianna pause. "At least you're seen. You have the choice to be solitary or not because they acknowledge that you have magic. You're taken seriously. You're a threat to them. That's why they pull out the big guns to deal with you, instead of pretending you're invisible."

All of Vianna's rage melted away in a wave of embarrassment. She sucked at being a friend. Dee had been completely disregarded, and Vianna had forgotten that fact, in a whole two seconds, because of her own seething rage for Charles. Dee hadn't been given a word or even a glance from the other witches. She'd been invisible, not even a factor to consider. That wasn't something a friend casually overlooked. Vianna needed to be a better friend.

"They're stupid. I'm stupid. You know that, right?" Vianna nudged Dee before they crossed the street to Tuck's shop. "You're just as powerful a witch as any of them. Probably even more so." Vianna believed that too.

"We don't know that." The tone of Dee's voice caused Vianna's chest to tighten. "And we never will. I'm not demon-bound, and we both know I'll never get the opportunity to be coven-bound. That means no magic for me."

"Dee..." Vianna wasn't sure what to say because technically Dee was right. She needed to be demon-bound or coven-bound in order to access magic, but that couldn't be the only answer. "You matter, and you *are* powerful. And eventually, every old hag of a witch in Salem is going to know it too."

Dee forced a smile and nudged her shoulders back. "And it's not like I don't have stuff in the works. I have a whole business plan to figure out for us with our paranormal investigation plans. We're gonna be legit."

They stopped in front of the shop, and Dee put a hand on her hip, nudging her satchel behind her. "Did Tuck give you more details? Ya know, more than bad mojo or whatever."

They would have to pick up the conversation of Dee and magic later because Vianna didn't have any answers. Not yet, at least. For the time being, she gladly jumped at a subject change.

"No. Just vagueness about ghosts and ill intentions. My plan is to take a peek, then get out. We're just here to gather info so *he* can figure out what to do. That's it." The old brass knob was cold under her palm, and the rusted entrance bell gave a well-used clank as she pushed the door open.

With a snort, Dee followed Vianna into the store. "What about Witches Be Bitches? Hmm. Or Fix Your Drama, Mama. No, that's too long and definitely gives the wrong impression. Our business name needs to sound tough but approachable."

"There's no sounding like anything." Vianna huffed as she closed the door to the busy street behind them. "We're doing a favor for a friend. That's it. Not officially investigating."

A heady aroma of angelica incense with an earthy undertone hung in the air, and Dee paused mid-brainstorming, raising a brow at Vianna. Angelica was commonly used to ward off evil and protect women or children. Ashley must really be spooked. That was unexpected and made Vianna take pause.

They wandered around a thick oak bookshelf in the middle of the shop, filled with bundled herbs and drawstring sacks. Small pegs lined the side facing them, and dolls with stitched *x*'s for eyes hung in shades of deep forest colors. They were grouped by hex flavor: memory, karma, truth, and the ever-popular love potion. They were no more effective than the dolls in the display case at the thrift shop. The real goods were in the back, but they only allowed locals behind that curtain. Vianna followed the sound of loud whispering, bumping into the hemp hamper filled with knotted scarves.

"Ruby, I *can't*. I should've said no before, but... I miss you. I thought we'd be able to talk. I thought if you saw me, you'd remember—"

A rapid tapping sounded. "No. You're not listening. I *can't*. Tuck is already going to murder me. Things have been really weird since you guys left."

Vianna wanted to groan. Ashley was clearly up to something, and the chances of this going quickly just flew out the door. But Vianna promised Tuck she'd look around, so she stepped from behind the shelving, Dee at her side, and approached the counter.

Instead of Ashley's usual costume of a top hat and corset vest that highlighted her ample cleavage, she wore flowing cotton and bone jewelry, and her black, silky hair was tied up in a mound of bouncy curls. Vianna suspected this look was more the real Ashley, and the other version was just for the tourists, but it was hard to tell because Ashley was a chameleon that played whatever part she needed in the moment.

Ashley's eyes widened at Vianna, and she stopped tapping her pen against the counter. "I gotta go." She pulled the phone from her ear.

Dee sauntered over, resting her elbows on the glass top, and Vianna rested a hip against the display. Neither said a word.

"Tuck isn't here." Ashley's eyes darted between both of them before settling on Dee. "Have we met?"

Dee shrugged, unfazed. "When Which Witch is called, you get both of us."

Vianna cringed at the name. They were getting progressively worse.

"It's a legal issue. Business partners and all. I'm Sandeen Layton. You must be Ashley."

Ashley pursed her lips into a tight scowl.

Vianna needed to push the conversation forward. "Tuck asked

us to stop by and check that everything is okay." Which it clearly wasn't, but Vianna wanted to see how Ashley framed the situation instead of putting words in her mouth.

"So, who's Ruby?" Dee grinned.

Ashley's cheeks and neck blossomed a soft red like a rose in the first stages of ripening, and her focus flicked briefly to her phone. She drummed the counter, blue paint caught in the cuticles of her chewed-down nails. "Nobody."

Ashley walked from behind the counter, her flowing crimson skirt tied in a knot between her deep-brown legs. She moved in front of the curtain that led to the back, blocking the hallway with her wide stance. "Tell Tuck everything is *fine*."

In all the times Vianna had come to the shop the past few months, Ashley had never once bothered to look up from her phone while perched behind the register. Yet, suddenly, here she was blocking the velvety barrier to the back of the shop.

Vianna let out a long breath. "I promised him I'd look around. So that's what I'm going to do."

Ashley folded her arms across her chest, unmoving. Nope, this would not be quick at all.

3

We Have Ghosts

Ashley didn't move, her stance broad and ready for battle. Vianna wasn't moving either, but she also was at a loss for what happened next. Not being a fist fight kind of girl meant that her lack luster intimidation tactics had been both plan A and B.

"That's cute." Dee brushed past them both, swiping the deep-blue curtain out of the way. "Yeah, we're not doing that. Sorry, not sorry."

Ashley squeaked in surprise, and Vianna scurried after Dee.

The narrow hallway was empty of ghosts, and when Dee pushed open the bathroom door, Vianna peeked in over her shoulder. Still no ghosts. With a shrug, Vianna moved to the next door, looking into Tuck's gaming cave, which was darker and cooler than the rest of the rooms. It was weird seeing all the monitors with black screens.

Dee nudged beside her into the doorway. "Anything?"

"Nope." Vianna turned back toward the hallway.

Ashley stomped toward them. "I'm not sure what you thought you were going to find."

Across from the gaming room was a walk-in closet with hinges but no door. Shelves covered the walls, packed full of blankets, mason jars of unknowns, bundles of wires, bricks, and old monitors. In the center of the floor, a blue-and-orange striped rug had been shoved aside to reveal an open trapdoor.

"That's just storage." Ashley tried to stand in their way, but Vianna and Dee skirted around her.

Vianna stopped at the edge of the opening, the tip of her boots beside a ladder that led into darkness. A cool wind drafted upward, and an answering warmth tingled within Vianna's fingertips. Shuck was making his curiosity known. She paused, listening for any noises, but there was only an eerie silence.

"This accesses the tunnels that run below Salem." Dee bounced on the balls of her feet, making the dangles on her ankle boots clatter.

"They're mostly blocked off," Ashley said. "There's nothing to see. I was just doing some cleaning."

Vianna noticed the bucket of blue paint by the trapdoor. The inside of the door had a glossy sheen, like it was still wet. "And painting."

Ashley straightened her bracelets, not making eye contact. "Just sprucing things up."

"Huh." Dee glanced around at the floor, probably noticing the same things as Vianna. Symbols that could have been from an antique compass were drawn in white chalk on the floorboards.

"That's haint blue, right?" Dee asked. "I read an article on that once, how, within hoodoo, haint-blue-painted doors protect against spirits. Someone's getting serious."

Vianna leaned back over the open hole, looking into the darkness, but didn't see any movement—ghost or otherwise.

"We're so going in the tunnels, aren't we?" Dee leaned over the opening with a large grin. Her energy matched Shuck's bubbling curiosity.

Vianna, instead, felt dread. The tunnels looked dark and cold. They were probably filled with bugs, not to mention the possibility of ill-intentioned ghosts. *Great.*

"You can't go down there." Ashley grabbed the trapdoor to pull it closed, but Vianna gripped the edge, stopping her.

"Clearly something is going on." Vianna tilted the door back against the wall and motioned to the symbols on the floor to prove her point. "And you know Tuck didn't just randomly ask me to stop by. He's hearing stuff. Whatever you have going on, you don't have it under control." She gave her best not-backing-down expression. It was the one she used with Grandma.

"This is none of your business, *witch.*" Ashley's upper lip twitched on the last word.

"Oh," Dee said, "it's gonna be like that? Fine. Since Tuck owns the shop, his word trumps yours. Why don't you busy yourself with the toys up front?" Dee made a shooing motion with her hand. "We've got this."

"Fine by me. I don't care if something happens to you. You're not my responsibility, but you should know those tunnels aren't stable." Ashley spun and marched from the closet, down the hallway.

Vianna tilted her head toward Dee. "How unstable?"

"We probably shouldn't over think that." Dee cringed. "Think of the ghosts you might see." Dee stood beside Vianna, both of them staring down at the black hole. "Famous figures like Elias Derby or George Washington."

Elias Derby was as much of a staple as George Washington in Salem classrooms. He was one of the first millionaires in the United States and had amassed his fortune from buccaneering before the Salem port was shut down to the public. The tunnels were originally commissioned by him and other ship captains to avoid paying taxes on their loot.

"It doesn't work like that. I only see a ghost if they died in that location. And I don't really want to see good old George or Elias in their final moments. Photos in history books are just fine."

It wasn't just the death loops in a dark and secretive tunnel system she was avoiding, but also the large bugs and rodents that probably had found cozy homes. Technically, Vianna had fulfilled her favor to Tuck. She could tell him that there was no ghost activity in the shop and that Ashley was likely messing around in the tunnels. Done and done. Vianna scrunched her face at her weak reasoning to bail. She'd like to think she'd learned to stop running. There was more intel to be found, and Tuck's whole life was this shop.

Vianna looked over the shelves. "See any flash lights?"

"No need." Dee held up her phone and swiped the screen.

Light blinded Vianna, and she raised a hand to shield her eyes. Dee redirected her phone to point at the opening, then immediately lowered her long bare legs into the darkness, one rung at a time, ruffled army-print skirt and all. "You coming?" she chirped right before dipping out of view.

Vianna tried to shake the bouncing energy from her hands and placed a foot on the first ladder rung. "How are you so excited about climbing into creepy-ass tunnels?"

"It's the adventure of it!" Dee sang out.

Damp darkness pressed against Vianna as she lowered herself, making her grateful that she wasn't claustrophobic. Pebbles crunched beneath her boots as she stepped from the ladder. She took a blind step forward and something scurried by her foot. She froze, every muscle held in place.

"Damn it," Dee said from somewhere in the darkness. "My phone stopped working."

"I can't see anything." Vianna fumbled in her pocket for her own phone, feeling for what side was up or down based on the volume buttons. "Where are you?"

"I think my phone went dead." Dee's voice came from a few feet away to the right. "It's not working at all, and I don't remember the last time I charged it."

A rock tumbled, followed by a smacking noise that echoed wetly.

"What was that?" Dee's voice was squeaky high.

The light from the trapdoor spotlighted the worn wooden ladder, revealing stains that Vianna hoped were dirt and not blood. Everything else was pitch-black. She stumbled with her phone, and it slipped from her fingers, then landed somewhere in the darkness with a *thump*. "Shit."

Trying not to think about the cost of fixing a cracked screen, she bent down, feeling around for the phone and whacking her elbow against something hard. She flinched from the sharp pain and bit back a yelp. Determined, she patted the ground around her feet and found nothing but dirt. She did larger sweeps outward, but still nothing.

"I swear something just bumped into my foot. Dear goddess, please be a mouse and not something worse. What are you doing?" Dee's voice moved to Vianna's left.

Another pat down of the ground, but still nothing. "I dropped my phone."

"You've got to be kidding me."

Vianna felt around, running into hard wood. After more blind groping, she realized it was a table leg with carved details like the antiques Mother had collected. Her phone was a lost cause. There had to be some sort of light source; it wasn't like there were windows. She followed the leg up until she found the top of a table, then felt around, looking for matches, a lantern, something from whoever was down here last. She found paper scraps, some sort of metal figurine, and then knocked over a glass bottle that rolled away and clanked against a rock. Dee made a startled yip.

"Sorry. That was me." Vianna's hand stopped on a plastic tube. She picked it up, feeling with both hands. It was a flashlight; she was sure of it.

She thumbed up the button on the side. Erratic flickers of light bounced against a battered desk, and she saw flashes of more paper scraps, cylinder blocks holding up a splintered piece of wood in a makeshift shelf, and more empty glass liquor bottles. She smacked the flashlight against the side of her leg, then tried again. The light still went in and out, flashing against the tunnel walls.

"Wait. Go back," Dee said. "There were candles."

Shaking the flashlight to make it work better, Vianna lifted the beam back to the wall. Sure enough, there was a carved-out ledge filled with half-burned black candles. Long wax fingers stretched into the cracks and down to a pile of rocks on the ground. Dee joined her, standing in front of the candles.

"Do you see matches?" Vianna asked while trying to peek behind the pillars. She saw a mirror, which was odd, but no matches.

"No," Dee said. "And what's the deal with that flashlight? It's like walking through one of those haunted mazes during Halloween."

"It's crap. That seems to be the deal." With no matches, Vianna shined the light at the ground as though her phone would magically appear. It didn't.

Her fingertips warmed, and her blood pulsed beneath her skin. Magic. Shuck was trying to tell her something. She narrowed her eyes at the candles. Matches weren't the only way to light a candle.

Magic was easier to pull on from within the house; everything had to do with proximity to Shuck. The further she was from him, the more she had to focus. At least, focus seemed to be the pivotal factor in her experiments over the past few months. She'd practiced lighting candles and making seeds sprout from different distances away from the house. There seemed to be no limit on how far she could go because of the magic itself, but the issue had more to do with how long or hard she could concentrate, keeping the connection between her and Shuck alive.

"What's with the dramatic pause?" Dee asked.

"I think I can light the candles." Vianna handed over the torch of sporadic, dull light. "Here, hold this for a minute."

She closed her eyes and took a deep breath, filling her lungs to capacity. Using magic in an unfamiliar place made her anxious because there were unknown factors for Shuck to tangle up with. She just needed to remind herself that she was in control, not him. He provided the magic, but she was the conduit, making her responsible for how the magic was funneled and directed. After one more deep breath, she opened her eyes and snapped her fingers. The clustered row of candles burst into flame.

"Let there be light," Dee whispered.

Vianna gave a proud nod. "And so it shall be." She turned around, and her grin sank.

She'd lit not only the small row of candles on the ledge but also every other candle in the large cavern and down the two tunnels that branched further out. Shuck never went halfway with anything. Noticing her phone in the dirt close to the stairs, she went and picked it up, slipping it into her back pocket.

Dee nodded to one of the tunnels. "I smell rose oil. And whiskey. At least under the dust and mildew."

"Me too," Vianna muttered. "Could be a group of Google witches. I saw a mirror behind the candles." Mirrors weren't exactly a staple for the craft, but that combined with the candles made it a possibility.

"Or it could be younger witches all riled up over the Mabon season and tonight's market," Dee said. "Although I don't know how anyone is getting around down here with all this junk."

She had a point. The small space was filled with discarded furniture, boxes, and even old bookshelves filled with yard sale rejects. They followed their noses and cautiously approached the tunnel, shimmying around stacks of crates and between wine barrels. Small flames flickered from clusters of candles on top of dressers and nightstands. Even a few glass lamps had woken to the call of magic.

The clutter thinned out as they moved deeper into the tunnels, and they could walk normally without having to squeeze through sideways past random chairs and boxes. The candles were sparse, but still better than the flashlight.

"See anything?" Dee asked. She gripped the strap to her satchel as they walked. "Any ghosts?"

"It's hard to tell down here." The corners were thick with shadows and further up there was more darkness than light. "But nothing to explain what Tuck said. Actually, nothing at all. I was expecting more ghosts. Or, at least, *some* ghosts." Or at least some evidence of why Ashley was painting haint blue on doors.

"Do you ever wonder why you can see ghosts?" Dee asked, her voice soft.

Vianna frowned. "Because I'm cursed?" She didn't really believe that, but sarcasm was the easiest reaction. Or maybe not, with Dee's answering silence. "Not really," she admitted. "Guess I kinda just focus on surviving with the hand I was dealt."

"It's crazy rare. I've only found two other cases of it in all of the coven records I've seen." Dee was silent again, and Vianna was beginning to suspect she was going somewhere with this.

"I also noticed—" Dee let out a long breath. "—that your father isn't recorded in the logs."

Vianna stopped walking and pivoted toward Dee. She did not like where this was going.

Dee stopped too, facing Vianna, eyes wide. Then the words started rushing out of her. "And that's just as rare. You know how witches are with logs. It seems like maybe your ghost stuff comes from your dad's side. Have you ever seen anything about him? Any reason why your mom would keep his identity from the coven?"

Vianna tightened her grip on the flashlight she still held. "I'm not one of your fun little research projects. You didn't even ask before digging into my personal life."

Vianna turned and stomped down the tunnel, away from the conversation.

"Vie," Dee shouted, jogging after her. "Hold up. I'm sorry. I just— Vie. Wait." Dee grabbed her arm and tugged her to a stop. "I know. I should have asked. I'm sorry. But not knowing means you don't understand everything you can do. You don't know potential weaknesses. There's a whole half of you we know nothing about. I think you should try to find out."

"Do you know your dad?" Vianna shot back. She'd never let herself even think about who her dad might have been. Never let herself hope he might have been different from her mother. Hope was scary—it made someone vulnerable to disappointment. "Why don't you look into your own shit?"

"I have," Dee said. "He died when I was little. I've traced his family line in Syria, and they're not interested in meeting me."

And another hit to the gut, followed by a wave of guilt. Vianna closed her eyes. "I'm sorry."

"It's okay," Dee said.

Vianna opened her eyes with a frown.

Dee gave her a weak smile. "I really should have asked first. But, you matter to me, Vie. I want to make sure we're prepared for whatever."

"I never wanted to know what happened to him because it likely would lead back to my mother, and that never goes well. I don't think I could handle discovering the death loop of my mother killing my father. Seeing what she did to Nancy..." Vianna shook her head. "I don't want to find more." And if that wasn't what had happened, then he'd left a baby to be raised by a killer. Neither option was worth pursuing. Maybe he was something even worse than Mother.

Dee gripped Vianna's arm. "I'm sorry."

Something rustled a few feet away, and they both froze. Slowly turning in the direction of the noise, Vianna noticed a tattered box on a three-legged chair propped against the tunnel wall. The box shifted again, and they both stepped backward, knocking over an old bicycle with a missing tire.

"Maybe we should just ignore it and keep going?" Vianna kicked her foot loose from the bicycle.

"And then have a mutant rat chase us down and chew off our toes?" Dee stepped closer to the box.

"A rat is preferable to some demon who's demented from being only partially summoned by Google witches who didn't know what they were doing." Vianna reluctantly followed Dee. There was an old water stain that spread up from the bottom of the box. The word Donations was scribbled in faded red marker on the side.

"That's not funny," Dee said. "What if there *is* some demented demon in there?"

"That's gotta be unlikely. Right?" Vianna asked.

They stood side by side, looking down at it. Only one flap covered the top. Neither of them moved to touch it. Something slammed the side of the box from the inside, and it flipped off the chair. A flash of gray flew at them. They both screamed. Vianna swatted at the air in defense, and fur collided with her arm midair, then flipped to the ground before darting into the tunnels. Vianna's hand was on her chest, and she took a deep breath, releasing the rush of nerves.

"Well, this is turning into a huge disappointment." Dee chuckled. "I wanted actual ghosts for our first official investigation. Not cats and Google witches."

"I'm good with cats." Vianna pushed forward further into the cavern.

The air grew frigid like an incoming frost storm. Tunnels were usually cold, being underground and all. And not every drop in temperature meant paranormal activity. But this was a polar drop within seconds. Vianna halted just inside the cavern, and Dee bumped into her back with an oof.

What Vianna saw wasn't just a single ghost, or even two or three, but a whole group of them. They were lounging over boxes, leaning against the walls, or passed out on the broken bed in the corner. They were women, every single one, and dressed in various ruffled skirts, loose chemises, and button-up ankle boots or hole-riddled stockings. A few held bottles of dark glass, and the space was saturated in the smell of rose oil and whiskey.

"Looks like you got your wish, Dee." Vianna rested a hand on her hip and looked around, trying to piece together what in Hades was going on. "We have ghosts."

4

⚬⚬⚬

Jammiest Bits of Jam

"What do you see?" Dee's breath came out in a white puff as she rubbed both her arms. "Don't hold back. I want every spooky detail."

"Well," Vianna began, "there's a group of all women, and they mostly seem to be hanging out."

"What? Where?"

Vianna opened her mouth to give more details, but Dee rattled off more questions, each faster than the one before.

"How did they die? Oh, were they all kidnapped and killed here? How long ago? Tell me it was a cult! That would be freaky."

Vianna pointed to a ghost with silver curls who sat on a crate. "That one is stitching clothes. She's older than the rest." She nodded to the pair in the corner. "They're throwing dice and are young. Super giggly. Also barely clothed." One was topless, wearing only stockings and panties, and the other was in a satin slip. Vianna pointed to the bed. "She's passed out in an unbuttoned blouse and hiked-up ruffled skirt. I'd guess 1800s-ish from the clothes."

"That doesn't sound like a kidnapping." Dee stepped further into the cavern. "The rose oil is crazy strong in here."

Warmth trickled up Vianna's spine, and she furrowed her brow, looking around. What had Shuck's attention?

A ghost with a long braid draped over her shoulder paused her feathered writing quill, looking up at Vianna with a grin. "You're a bricky little thing. Half off?" She tugged at the knotted ribbon of her chemise as she hummed.

The ghost continued to focus on Vianna. "Blessed be to things of flesh that warm between thy thighs—for lips that look of sweetness like candied apple pie, for curves to tame as wild as a tide rising high, and for promises that beckon like sparkles within thine eyes."

"Hush your sass-box, Larissa," said the ghost with silver curls.

The poetry ghost smirked as she flicked her braid over her shoulder. "Oh, come now, we all know I have the jammiest bits of jam."

"You're not on until sunset. Rest." The other ghost didn't look up from the pile of worn fabrics in her lap, a needle pinched between her wrinkled fingers.

"Why is your face doing that?" Dee asked.

Vianna scowled, now at both Dee and the ghost. "Doing what? It's my face."

"It's all scrunched up. Something's up. Dish." Dee tilted her head as she stared at Vianna.

"They're reciting dirty nursery rhymes. At least, I think that's what it was."

"Oh, you better remember that little nugget, 'cause I'm asking later."

The amount of awareness from the ghosts was similar to Grandma, but Grandma had a couple of centuries on them. Plus, the whole being-a-witch thing made her more coherent than other ghosts her age. But this gathering didn't quite check the boxes for a coven.

"Has there ever been some kind of underground brothel in the tunnels?" Vianna asked.

"Brothel?" Dee twirled, eyes wide, as though if she could squint hard enough she'd see the ghosts. "Our first case, and we have not only *real* ghosts but brothel ghosts!"

Being able to see ghosts wasn't the fantasy Dee imagined it to be, but at least these brothel ghosts were less gory than most. A whole lot less, now that Vianna thought about it. How *had* they died? And why weren't they caught in a death loop?

"They don't match the ill-intentioned description from Tuck." Vianna gestured toward another tunnel. "Let's see if there's something in the next cavern."

They squeezed through towers of stacked bricks before finding another cavern. Two ghosts were in a sword duel. Well, almost a sword duel. One had a dagger and, despite the disadvantage, did a twist around and slammed the blade into the chest of his opponent, but he'd let down his guard, and a sword protruded from his own gut. They slumped into the dirt together, almost synchronized, their knees slamming into the dirt first and then their bodies collapsing into a heap. They stared at one other with narrowed eyes full of rage as life drained from them, and then the emptiness that Vianna saw so often replaced the rage.

Dee nudged her. "More prostitutes?"

"No." Vianna shook her head. "Just the standard stray ghosts you'd expect in a place like this. Nothing that we're looking for."

"It's warmer in this cavern." Dee rubbed her hands together. "Let's do some sleuthing!"

More clues weren't the worst idea. They poked at clusters of junk in stacked crates and then looked through more trinkets on a leaning bookshelf. Long-forgotten candlesticks, ripped books, baby bottles, and clothes weren't exactly a jackpot of information.

"There's nothing here. The brothel ghosts are the biggest anomaly, but I don't think it's what Tuck is looking for. Maybe there's something up top that I missed."

Dee pushed out her lips in a pout. "Boo. Okay, back up we go."

They headed in the direction they came, down the tunnel and toward the next cavern with the brothel ghosts. The air grew heavy with rose oil like before, but also a hint of smoke. "Do you smell that?" Vianna looked around, checking to see if the smell was part of the ghosts or an actual fire.

"Rose oil," Dee asked. "Yeah, it's all over down here."

"No, there's more. Smoke."

They reentered the brothel cavern, but this time, the ghosts didn't acknowledge them, didn't play dice, and didn't sew ripped clothing. They were huddled together, all looking at the same spot on the wall, hands pressed to their mouths. Vianna's eyes burned at the edges, and she blinked, then squinted, looking around. The cavern felt hazy, and each inhale made her throat tickle.

"Something is different." Vianna's heart thumped harder. The air was heavy, and she knew she was seeing something from long ago. A death loop. She counted her breaths—*one, two, three*—trying to keep each breath calm and steady. Not real. Whatever was coming, it was not real.

"It's North-Pole-freezing, but looks the same to me." Dee frowned at her.

Vianna knew she should explain. Say more. But she just kept counting in her head. *Four. Five.* It was cold. Really cold. *Six. Seven.* A sudden burst of fire needles tried to break through her fingertips from the inside out, creating a pulsing pressure. A low animal growl shook her chest. She coughed at the growing scratch in her throat and blinked back the burning tears from smoke that wasn't there. Between Shuck and the death loop, she didn't know where to focus.

"Larissa! Get away from the door. Hurry!" The older brothel

ghost corralled the others away from the wall now leaking tendrils of smoke.

Vianna rubbed her eyes, her eyelids feeling like sandpaper on the inside. Smoke filled the cavern, and she raised her sleeve to cover her nose and mouth, backing away. She plastered herself against a wall, coughing into her sleeve.

"Vie, what's wrong?" Dee's voice called from somewhere, but all Vianna could see were thick clouds of smoke and ash. The brothel ghosts screamed calls for help as they pounded against the walls.

Her fingers felt like they were made of fire, spreading up her arms and into her collarbone. Was ghost-fire consuming her or was Shuck trying to take over? She held the burning tight within her, not letting it free in case it was Shuck. She didn't know what he would do, and she wouldn't let anyone get hurt, especially Dee.

The cries for help turned into guttural wailing that sent shivers through Vianna's bones. They were burning alive. The cavern seemed to shrink, as though the walls could move and press in on her. Each gasp of breath clogged her airway with more smoke. Vianna clawed at her neck and chest.

"Vianna!" Dee was yelling now.

Poetry Ghost dropped to her knees as a backdrop of flames roared behind her and up her back. Fire engulfed the long braid draped over her shoulder. "Trapped," the ghost gurgled. Her ear melted from the heat, stretching to her shoulder like wax. She staggered closer to Vianna. "Everyone. Trapped."

Vianna pressed her back against the rock, raising her arms as a shield. A searing pain wrapped around her arm as the ghost latched onto her with claw like hands. Vianna screamed.

An arm wrapped around her waist, and she was yanked to her feet, then dragged from the cavern. It was only as they passed through the furniture-riddled tunnel, when the air cleared, that she realized Dee was the one pulling her. Vianna pushed herself away and stood on her own two feet. After a few deep gasps, she stopped coughing, and her throat no longer burned.

"What kind of haunted fun show was that?" Dee asked.

Vianna leaned against the wall as she relished full, deep breaths, smoke-free. "Death loop. Sometimes I get pulled into them. It takes a strong ghost. Usually the ghost of a witch."

Dee shook her head with a frown. "Come on, let's get out of here."

Wrapping her arm around Vianna once again, Dee walked them back to the first cavern. The candles were still lit, the smell of fire was gone, and rose oil faintly lingered.

"The brothel must have caught fire. The girls were burned alive." Vianna closed her eyes against the memory of the poetry girl reaching for her. She could still feel the searing grip of her hand.

"But there haven't been any fires down here," Dee said. "I'd have read something, and there would be evidence of fire damage, even if it happened centuries ago."

"They were staring at the wall like something was on the other side. Like it was a window or door. It doesn't make any sense. I've never seen ghosts relive their death loop in a different location than where they died."

"Your arm," Dee barked. "Since when can ghosts *burn* you?"

Vianna looked down to see her sweater burned through, and the exposed skin of her forearm a puffy, bright red. "I... I..." she stuttered. "I don't know." And it *hurt*.

"I don't like this." Dee got behind her and nudged her toward the ladder. "It's time to go."

Vianna used her non-burned arm to hold her weight as she climbed up and out, Dee following right behind. When they emerged from the back of the shop, two giggling teenagers were leaving, rummaging through black gift bags with the *Sticks and Bones* logo. Ashley sat behind the register, speaking into her phone.

"You can't come tomorrow." She tugged at a lock of hair by her ear. "What if Tuck comes home early? That's cutting it too close. *I can't.*"

Dee cleared her throat, and Ashley jumped to her feet, slamming her phone against the counter. "You're back."

Vianna moved her burned arm behind her. "Someone has been messing around down there."

They hadn't found anything stationary to tell Tuck, and a slipped hint from Ashley would be really helpful. "Anything you want to let us know?"

"There's nothing to tell." Ashley put a hand on her hip, looking like the perfect picture of someone who wasn't afraid of Vianna one bit.

Vianna reminded herself that Tuck liked Ashley. He claimed she had a sixth sense that couldn't be taught. He hadn't just hired her because she was his cousin; he'd hired her for her potential. She certainly had moxie. Vianna could see that.

"Those tunnels run for miles with countless access points all across Salem." Ashley shrugged. "Anything could've happened down there, but *I* haven't been in the tunnels. So, like I said, there's nothing to tell on my end."

"But your trapdoor was open," Vianna said.

Ashley raised a brow. "I know you're witches, but come on. You saw that I was painting. Surely you know that the right blend of haint blue can act as protection when on the outer part of the door. I don't know who called Tuck, but he should have called *me*, not you. I'm well aware of the negative energy, and I'm handling it. Without *your* kind."

Vianna couldn't fault Ashley for being anti-witch. The whole lot of them weren't exactly pillars of greatness or do-gooders within the community.

"Well," Dee said. "We'll let you get back to it because we have somewhere to be. See you around, Ashley." Dee tugged Vianna by the elbow of her not-burned arm and headed toward the exit.

"I hope not," Ashley snarked at their backs.

Once outside, Dee led the way to an alleyway between two brick buildings, avoiding the remaining clusters of political crowds dressed in red, white, and blue. When they reached the Jeep, Dee acted like a nurse on the battlefield, grabbing Vianna's arms and yanking different ointments and wraps from her satchel. They were both quiet as she worked, spreading goop, then wrapping the burn.

"That actually feels better. Thank you," Vianna said.

Dee finished tucking her supplies back into the satchel. "I'm going to ignore the 'actually' part of that statement. You're welcome."

Vianna grinned. "Double-y thanks."

"What happened down there? Has a ghost ever been able to physically hurt you like that?"

"No." Vianna huffed. "And I've never seen a death loop in a different location than where it happened." Even Grandma Susannah, as old as she was and being a demon-bound witch, didn't leave her death location. She'd been hanged on the property and stayed on the property.

"Are we sure they're not a coven?" Dee put her first aid gear away and started the Jeep. "The ghost of a witch is stronger, right? That would track with what happened to your arm."

"I guess they could have been a coven and working at a brothel. We have pirate covens, after all."

Dee put the Jeep in drive. "I need to stop for gas on the way home."

They headed onto Essex Street as Vianna replayed everything that happened in the tunnels and everything Tuck had said. They pulled into the gas station, and Dee hopped out to fill the tank. Vianna got out and tapped the hood. "Want anything from inside?"

Dee looked over. "The usual. But none of that clearance-basket crap you always get. It's not a bargain when it tastes old and warped."

Vianna grinned as she headed toward the convenience store. "One load of clearance candy coming up."

The glass door was stiff as she jerked it open, then stumbled inside. The cashier was a thin, balding white man, and he chuckled along with a familiar figure at the counter. Vianna's gut tightened. Charles.

She darted to her left, down an aisle, and pretended to be interested in travel-size packets of Aspirin and Midol. Maybe he didn't see her. A pungent combination of dirt and toilet bowl cleaner saturated the store.

"Mr. Barton," the cashier said. "I just want you to know that you've got my vote, sir. And my family's votes. Hell, we'll even sneak the teenager into one of them booths. And anyone else who will listen to me."

Vianna rolled her eyes as she meandered down the aisle. The large refrigerators filled with colored drinks hummed.

"I very much appreciate the support, Paul." Charles was loud, projecting so anyone in the store could hear him. "You're good people, but don't be getting that young daughter of yours into trouble."

Vianna did her best to ignore the conversation, heading up a new aisle and perusing the rows of brightly colored candy bags.

"It's a real shame what happened to your ma," the cashier said. "Them cults over there in that part of town have been a problem for a long time. I heard they peddlin' drugs out of them old houses. Throwing parties to recruit new drug mules and pull in the young girls. It ain't right. And I heard your mama was trying to clean that area up. We know she comes from the right side of the law. You come from good people."

He glanced over his shoulder at Vianna, flashing a quick grin, then focused his oozing fake charm on the cashier. So he did know she was there. *Great.*

"You're right, Paul. I do care about Salem, just like my mama cared. And I'm gonna finish what she started." Charles handed over a credit card.

Paul the cashier waved the card away. "Your money ain't no good here. Your gas is on us. What you said about every person being seen, it meant something to those of us scraping by on an honest living. Me and my family will do everything we can to help."

Vianna froze, her outstretched hand holding a bag of Skittles. She knew she was out of touch with the non-magical citizens of Salem, but this was some impressive story twisting. Rose Barton was not a victim. And neither she nor Charles Barton were cleaning up anything in Salem. But people saw what they wanted to see.

Those not raised in the craft had a hard time seeing it. Most things could be explained away if one tried hard enough. It didn't matter if it was logical or not, because magic and demons were always less logical than any alternative. Accusations of cults or drugs were nothing new for the witch community, and the witches, if anything, found it amusing—since their crimes were far worse.

"You're a good man." Charles patted the counter. "I'll make sure my mother hears of your support during my next visit."

So he'd been visiting mother dearest at the Danvers State Hospital. "I'll tell her you said hello, too, Vianna." Charles turned from the counter to face her.

Vianna put the candy back. She'd shop elsewhere. "Yeah, you do that. Actually, maybe I should swing by myself." She had a few questions for Rose about the missing grimoire page.

"That won't be necessary." Charles's tone hardened, his smarmy smile slipping. She seemed to have that effect on him.

"Hmmm. Well. One never can tell." Vianna walked out of the store with her heart pounding. She refused to look over her shoulder to make sure he wasn't following her. They were in public, and he had an image to maintain. But she quickened her step regardless.

"Where's the goods?" Dee asked.

Vianna slid into the Jeep. "Let's get out of here. I'll tell you on the way home."

5

Crystal Grids

They turned onto Heritage Way, into the heart of the old witch neighborhood. As they approached the Roots house, Vianna saw a figure lingering outside the wrought iron fence that lined the front yard. It was her neighbor, Ophelia.

Dee pulled into the driveway and put the Jeep in park, then shifted toward Vianna with a raised brow. "Were you expecting company?"

"I don't think so."

Vianna leaned around Dee to take another look. Ophelia was mother to the Lunar Coven, and although they were friendly with one another, it was a rarity for Ophelia to pay a visit.

Vie climbed out of the car. "You know, you don't have to linger outside the fence like a burglar. The porch swing is crazy comfy now. Dee changed out the crusty cushions that were older than Grandma Aileen." Grandma Aileen was Mother's mother and had died long before Vianna was born.

"Aileen was almost as awful as your mother." The layered fabrics of Ophelia's dress flitted in the breeze, but her large afro didn't move.

Vianna should probably be offended by the dig at her mother, but she couldn't argue against any of it. And Ophelia wasn't trying to pick a fight; she was simply stating facts they both knew.

Dee opened the front gate, stalling with her hand on the iron handle. "Ophelia, are you still good to bring cornbread to the Mabon feast this weekend?"

Dee's impending feast was growing in size, along with Vianna's anxiety. She hoped Shuck would behave with that many people in the house. Company that didn't lose their body parts was an adjustment for him.

"I'll be there." Ophelia nodded, jingling the cascade of black obsidian stones that hung from her ears down to her shoulders. Obsidian was used in high-level wards of protection. Choosing those earrings meant something when it came to witches. Something was up.

"The Lunar's Mabon feast isn't until later that night. I'll have plenty of time to stop by and maybe pick up an extra batch of that Mabon cider of yours."

Dee beamed. A coven mother requesting her cider was a high compliment. "That can be arranged." She headed through the arch in the fence, jogged up the porch steps, and went inside.

Ophelia clasped her hands in front of her. "Last night was the fourth dark moon where my crystal grid wouldn't align. Something is disrupting it."

Vianna waited for more information, but there was only silence, minus the croaking frogs from the shadows under the shrubs, which had increased substantially since the assault by the Ramsey twins during the Original Blood Coven attack. Thankfully, none of the remaining frogs seemed poisonous, but instead were doing wonders at keeping the garden healthy.

Ophelia seemed far more comfortable in the stillness than Vianna. She didn't fidget, didn't second-guess where she was standing or where to put her hands. Knowing nothing about the crystal grid, Vianna stayed quiet. She stood beside Ophelia, looking forward and trying to see the house as she did. It looked better than a few months ago: the yard was weed-free, the thick layer of dust on the windows cleaned—except the attic window, but that was on her to-do list—the muck and spiderwebs dusted from the crevices, and she'd even managed a fresh sealant on the deck and porch swing.

She rocked from her heels to her toes, then back again. "So... a broken crystal grid means..."

"It means there's a disruptive energy. And in this case, the disruption is likely from the north-facing side of the grid, since that's the faulty connection." Ophelia turned to Vianna, arms folded over her chest. "Something is amiss with the northern property touching mine."

"I see." Vianna nodded.

Ophelia's northern neighbor was Vianna. She knew that much, but it was less clear as to what exactly was amiss. Answers weren't going to be found on the outside of her fence. She strolled through the archway, hoping Ophelia would follow.

"Got any other clues for me?" Something far less ominous would be helpful. The Lunar Coven was known for their uncanny seeing abilities, but also for their fortune cookie communication.

"Corruption comes in all forms," Ophelia answered as she followed onto the property. "What happened to your lawn?"

Vianna stopped mid-step up the porch and turned back. She knew the area Ophelia was referring to without turning around. A stretch of dirt arched in a half circle in the middle of the thick green grass. It was the bane of her existence. Before the dirt, there'd been straw grass that was *dead* dead, no matter what she'd tried. She'd raked at the straw, fertilized the soil with limestone, laid fresh seed, but nothing took.

Ophelia walked along the outer edge of the dirt arc with a deep frown that pushed her lower lip out and furrowed her brows. She fiddled with the chunk of amethyst that dangled from the chain around her neck. "There's an energy here, pushing me back. This isn't normal witchcraft."

No, it wasn't. "Let's just remember that I had a coven attacking my house. One of the four oldest covens in Salem, and arguably the most deadly." Vianna's words came out in a fast defensive blurt. "I wasn't in a position to turn down help. Even from a horrible source."

Ophelia's voice lowered. "What source?"

"Well..." Vianna twirled her thumb ring. "He claims to be a hoodoo practitioner, but I'm not sure if that's true, because Tuck says the hoodoo community shunned him ages ago."

Ophelia let out a long breath. "What sort of help did this shunned hoodoo practitioner offer?"

"War water." Vianna scrunched her nose. "Dee and I used it alongside a spell for a ward." She swallowed the lump in her throat. It really had seemed like the best plan at the time.

"A ward against witches?" Ophelia said. "Your own kind."

"Not exactly." Vianna cringed. "It was supposed to be specifically OBC witches. The coin at the bottom of the jar was even etched with that focal point."

Ophelia stood over the upturned soil. "Hmmm..."

Vianna already had a growing unease about the mark on the lawn, and this wasn't helping. "Do you think this is what's messing up your crystals?"

"It seems likely." Ophelia toed a clump of dirt with the tip of her boot. "Unless you have other *gifts* around the property from strange practitioners?"

"No," Vianna said. Tuck didn't count as strange, so the broom was good. Probably.

Ophelia narrowed her eyes at Vianna, clearly reading the hesitation on her face. "Child, there's a responsibility that comes with your familiar and his location, coven-bound or not. I've heard you're not pledging. Is that for sure?"

Vianna folded her arms over her chest. "I'm not joining the Original Blood Coven."

Ophelia unhooked a stone from one of her earrings and knelt at the edge of the soil. "What about another coven?"

That question was a surprise. Vianna straightened. She hadn't considered pledging to a different coven. Even when she'd run from her heritage, hiding in a city where her name didn't matter, she'd still practiced the craft. She was undeniably a witch. Knowing she wouldn't join the OBC didn't automatically mean she couldn't ever be coven-bound. Did it? The conversation with Dee earlier rattled in her mind. Vianna was seen and acknowledged by all covens, and it gave her options not everyone had. It wasn't fair, but it was true. Regardless of whether the covens saw or acknowledged Dee, Vianna did.

"My coven is Dee," Vianna said.

"I suspected as much." Ophelia buried the obsidian into the grass-less soil. "This isn't just a ward, child. It's a doorway that's leaking dark energy. What is the name of this helpful *friend*?"

He was anything but a friend. "Csada Laguerre."

"You'll need to buy more obsidian to soak up the energy until we can come up with a plan." Ophelia stood, wiping the dirt from her skirts. "Check your grimoire, and I'll ask around about this Csada."

Vianna looked down at the dirt, then at Ophelia as she tried to digest everything. "I need you to be direct. You're saying the war water wasn't just a ward, but a doorway? For... what? Csada? What does that mean?"

Ophelia wiped the last of the dirt from her hands. "You're asking me? I'm not the one who accepted maybe-hoodoo magic and soaked it into her yard." She tapped her temple with a finger. "You're smarter than this."

"They were trying to take Shuck. I was desperate." Vianna clamped her mouth shut, frustrated. This was not her shining moment.

"Yes, and what do you think this Csada is trying to take?" Ophelia didn't wait for Vianna to answer. She turned and sauntered across the lawn. She was right. Csada had declared his intentions to Vianna. He wanted the house. He wanted Shuck.

"Oh, and... " Ophelia stopped with a hand on the gate, speaking over her shoulder. "Tell Dee I did end up having an available booth for tonight. She inquired whether all of the allotted booths for the Lunar Coven were filled. As it so happens, we have *one* extra, and I reserved it for you two."

Vianna watched Ophelia make her way down the sidewalk toward her own home. A booth. At the witch market. Vianna couldn't wipe the grin from her face even if she wanted to. She might be scowled at by every legacy witch in attendance, but there was plenty of new blood and solitary witches to buy her products that were currently overflowing from the candle den. She almost hopped with excitement.

Vianna gave another look at the dirt in the yard that was somehow a ward *and* a portal—or something-something. She shook her head. Dirt had never been so confusing. A jolt of tingles pooled in her fingertips, and she looked back at the house. Shuck was up to something. She clamped down on the magic within her, imagining a mental vault with the door firmly shut. If she opened the door, there was no predicting what he'd do. He was too old and too powerful, and—if she was being fully honest with herself—she was too scared.

The marking on her collarbone flared with heat, and a loud snap came from within the house. That didn't sound like the standard old house groan. She tilted her head, breath held, waiting for what came next. And then she heard it: the sound of gushing water like a broken dam.

"Curse the goddess." She jogged up the porch stairs and slammed face-first into the front door. With a growl, she kicked the house. "This again? You're gonna throw a fit because I didn't let you play in the weird dirt?"

She also didn't let him fight the squirrel, inform the mailman he was to leave the mail outside the property fence, stretch out feelers during the moon phases, or mingle with the ghosts in the tunnels. They'd been having some trust issues.

The knob twisted open, and Vianna charged in, almost colliding with Dee, who tore down the stairs. They both whipped around the banister, toward the geyser of water shooting from the downstairs bathroom.

"Oh." Dee slid to a halt. "That's not good."

Vianna raised her voice to compete with the gushing water. "Shuck, that is enough."

He had full control over his pipes and their functions, and she wasn't under any delusions that this wasn't on purpose. The geyser shot higher.

"This is you two fighting?" Dee raised a palm to stop the splattering water. "Not my favorite."

Vianna mimicked Dee's hand-shield as she attempted to look at the damage in the bathroom. "The water is coming from where the sink handle is supposed to be." She wanted to kick the wall, but that wasn't going to help anything.

"You're only damaging yourself," Vianna yelled at the water. "It's gonna seep into your floorboards, and then you'll grow mold!" She didn't really know if that was true or not, but it was the first threat that came to mind. There weren't a lot of cards to play in a battle with a house. And since they were already bonded, there was no escaping each other. They would have to find some sort of truce.

Water rained down on them as Vianna turned to Dee. "I don't suppose you have experience with replacing sink handles?"

"I think we need to turn off the water first. I'll check YouTube." Dee jogged into the kitchen and out of the indoor storm.

Considering Shuck was fully capable of turning the water on or off, Vianna wasn't sure how much YouTube was going to help. Unless there were tutorials on bribing your possessed house to behave, because training him to do anything seemed out of the question.

Someone pounded on the front door, and for half a beat, Vianna froze. Whoever it was had the worst timing ever, and she wasn't about to let Shuck's tantrum go on display. Prioritizing the water over the front door, she forged into the bathroom. The sink handle to the right was still attached, and she twisted it both ways, but the water didn't stop.

A boulder of a black man nudged her out of the way and dove beneath the sink.

"What the—" she sputtered as water sprayed everywhere. "Grayson?"

His back muscles shifted beneath the quickly soaked, gray t-shirt as his head disappeared under the sink. The water gave another surge, splattering the ceiling. Vianna hunched as a bucket-load dumped on her, and then she gasped. It was freezing.

The water from the hole where the sink handle had been shrank until it was a small gurgling stream, then turned off entirely. Grayson gripped the edge of the sink and pulled himself up, an amused expression lighting up his face.

"Is there some magic make-it-stop button down there?" Vianna flicked water with her fingers.

"Actually, there is." Grayson wrung out his shirt, a small smile tugging one corner of his full mouth. "I turned off the water."

"I did that." Vianna frowned at the broken handle. "Or tried."

He pointed at the cabinet beneath the sink, then wiped the water from his neck. "There's always a spigot under a faucet to turn off the water." His attention flicked to her arm. "You okay?"

She hadn't changed from the oversized torn sweater that felt like a billion pounds now that it was wet. Glancing down, she realized her burn mark wasn't looking any better. "Yeah, I'm fine." She swiped a tangle of wet hair from her eyes and immediately regretted it when her sweater slopped more water in her face. "Where did you come from, anyway?"

"The front door." He was completely straight-faced, and she couldn't tell if he was being a smart-ass or just answering her dumb question. "I knocked several times. There was a lot of yelling, so I came in."

Dee stood in the archway to the kitchen with a hand on her hip, her expression mirroring exactly how Vianna felt. Since when did Shuck just let people in? Well, besides Dee, but Dee was Dee. Grayson was an unknown and, worse, a cop.

Shuck was oddly quiet. Grandma too.

"I need to clean up this mess." Vianna squeezed past Grayson, inhaling a lungful of spicy musk and ignoring the brief press of his bicep against her shoulder.

Shaking her head, she focused on what needed to be done, and that was getting towels for the new indoor pool.

"How about a drink?" Dee turned and sauntered into the kitchen.

"Sounds great." Grayson headed after her.

Vianna unloaded towels from the linen closet and unfolded them onto the floor like puzzle pieces. Shuck rumbled in her bones, and she sucked in her breath, dropping the last towel. Acting up in front of a cop was not what she needed right now. *Please chill out*, Vianna pleaded. There was no response, no tingling fingers, no warmth lacing through her veins or fire on her collarbone. Maybe silence was the best she could currently hope for. That didn't say a whole lot about their bond.

Vianna pulled off her waterlogged sweater and tossed it into the washroom beneath the stairs. She pulled on a t-shirt from the dryer and joined them in the kitchen. Dee bustled between the pantry and counter, hovering over the large pot on the stovetop. Grayson sat at the small dining table with mismatched chairs, choosing the cherry-wood Windsor, which put his back to the fridge and gave him a view of both the back door and the archway into the living room.

Grayson rested his elbows on the table, linking his fingers together. "I came to offer you a job."

Vianna paused, speechless. He wanted to hire a witch? Cops didn't work with witches. Maybe he had some weird fungus between his toes that needed heavy-duty witchery cream to vanquish. Someone that hot had to have a hidden downside. She managed to stutter out a chuckle. "A job doing what?"

"Confidential informant." He didn't miss a beat, spitting it right out as though it weren't the craziest idea she'd ever heard.

"You can't be serious."

"How much?" Dee asked at the same time.

"You can charge per case," Grayson said, unflinching.

Vianna stared at him. He was serious.

6

Ghost Exposure

"You're high." Vianna pulled out the chair across from Grayson and sat down. "You would have to be to ask a *witch* to work with a *cop*."

Law enforcement wasn't a part of the witch community. They fit in with the non-magic folks, giving the general public the feeling that their own could keep them safe. But Grayson had proven differ-ent. In the first month of coming home, Vianna had called the cops twice for a dead body—in her defense, only one was actually dead—and both times she'd called, Grayson had shown up. He'd made it abundantly clear that he recognized Vianna's house as a witch resi-dence, as well as the whole neighborhood. He knew witches were real. Whatever he was, it straddled the line between those who knew of magic and those who didn't.

He sat back in his chair. "You're uniquely qualified to work as an informant."

Dee slid three steaming mugs on the table, one for each of them, and sat in the cream-upholstered chair.

Vianna digested what he was suggesting, pausing a little too long before replying. "Uniquely qualified how?"

His lips spread into a full-on smile, and it was a good one, all pearly white and broad. He'd baited her into asking him more, proving she was interested. But she wasn't. She didn't think. Maybe. How much did a consultant get paid?

"You're demon-bound." He leaned forward, cupping the mug in front of him.

"He's been spying on you. You mustn't trust his Banbury tales." Grandma's scratchy voice came from behind Vianna in the living room, and it took effort not to turn toward her. Since when did Grandma keep her distance?

Although overly dramatic, Grandma had a point. Witches couldn't tell if someone was demon-bound just by looking at them or being around them. So how was *he* able to? She highly doubted he was *spying* on her, but he'd clearly done his homework. Grayson tilted his head, studying Vianna and making her self-conscious. There was way too much going on in those eyes. Had she flinched or made some movement at Grandma's voice?

He continued. "You're a legacy witch who calls the cops instead of burying bodies."

She raised a brow in challenge. "Maybe I bury *some of the bodies*, then call the cops for the excess. My property is only so big."

He traced the rim of his mug with his thumb but didn't break eye contact. "Maybe, but my gut says you're one of the good guys, and my gut is rarely wrong."

Dee gave a little hum as she sipped her coffee, and Grandma gave a snort from the living room. Vianna just stared. *Good guys?* For someone who claimed to know what a legacy witch was, there were some large gaps in his knowledge. Legacy witches were never the good guys, not a single one.

"My ears on the streets also say you come and go at a local hoodoo shop. From what I'm seeing, the social boundaries of Salem don't apply to you, giving you a unique ability to go wherever you want." He took a sip of the steaming drink, then coughed into his fist.

Vianna sucked in her lips to avoid chuckling. Dee had been testing different ciders for the Mabon feast, and they all had one thing in common: they were as strong as Mother's moonshine.

"No comments from you?" Vianna asked a grinning Dee.

"Nope." She wiggled into her chair and took a delicate sip from her own mug. "Officer Elliott seems to be doing just fine on his own."

Grayson pushed his mug further away and placed his clasped hands on the table. "We're getting reports of disturbances in the tunnels below town. Two shops have complained. Some of the others won't talk to me. That's where you would come in. All you have to do is gather intel, report it back to me, then collect a check."

"The tunnels?" Dee straightened. "Must be fate because we were in the tunnels this morning. In fact, I think that makes us *highly valuable* consultants. Ya know, the ones that get the big checks."

Grayson shook his head. "I don't want you *in* the tunnels or anywhere else with potential danger. Just gather intel *outside* the tunnels. You two are to avoid engaging with anyone dangerous or the actual crime scenes."

He was being a little naive. If he wanted someone who could go places he couldn't, it would involve danger in a variety of forms. But that was beside the point. "Let's not get ahead of ourselves. No one agreed to anything. And we don't work for you, so we go where we please."

Grayson made eye contact with Vianna, the serious stare-you-down-and-intimidate-you type. She held his stare, not looking away or backing down.

He spoke first. "Did you find anything in the tunnels?"

Dee tapped her manicure against the table, long, sharp-tipped nails coated in maple leaves and glitter. "Candles and such. There's still more intel to gather."

"Candles and such," Grayson repeated. "I'm assuming your access point was Sticks and Bones?"

"The owner called. He's out of town and asked me to stop by," Vianna said. "Which two stores called in complaints?"

"Books and Nooks and the Bee's Garden. The two shops on—" Grayson broke off when Dee finished the rest of his sentence.

"On each side of Sticks and Bones." Dee was all but bouncing in her chair.

"Exactly," he murmured.

"What kind of complaints?" Dee stood, taking her mug to the counter. She filled the kettle with water and turned a burner on.

"Not much." Grayson was still studying Vianna like he could pull thoughts from her head if only he could focus hard enough. "Nothing about *candles and such.*"

Vianna tilted her head and leveled a fake scowl at him. He wanted intel before he gave anything up. She didn't exactly blame him. "Candles and such was a subtle way of referencing Google or outcast witches. The tunnels are a great location for a gathering, but we didn't find anything that supported witch activity."

"We'll have more intel after tomorrow night." Dee dropped a pouch of tea into her mug.

Grayson tilted his head. "Tomorrow night?"

Dee turned to Vianna with an *oopsie* cringe face. Vianna mouthed *blabbermouth.*

"Tomorrow works for me." He slid his chair back and stood.

"We didn't agree to working together, and Tuck didn't give me permission to bring in the police." Vianna stood, following Grayson's lead.

He gave a shrug and headed toward the door. "Up to you if you want to get paid or not. Either way, I'll see you at *Sticks and Bones* tomorrow. Sundown?" He paused at the door, his fingers wrapped around the knob.

Shuck's rumble echoed through Vianna's chest, then spread outward through her limbs. It was different from his usual grumbles, as though he whispered a foreign language, and for half a second, she wondered if he was talking to someone other than her. Or maybe he was just warning her.

Grayson patted the door, pausing, his gaze searching Vianna's face. "I think we'd make a good team. Give it a shot."

He didn't wait for an answer and let himself out, closing the door behind him. Vianna stood there, unsure how she felt. She didn't team up with people. Then again, she had with Dee. And while her gut wasn't some special good-guy detection device like Grayson's seemed to be, he didn't set off any of her alarms.

"Did you notice that man's lips? I almost missed them, being distracted by his—"

"Dee!" Vianna laughed. She'd definitely noticed his lips, though. Full and soft looking. And his ass.

"I was going to say super sexy brain. Your mind is in deliciously dirty places."

"Sure you were," Vianna said. "Besides, he's a cop. There's a whole shelf of logs in the coven caves about how well witches and cops get along."

"So?" Dee stood by Vianna in the archway. "It's not like you're a coven-bound witch who adheres to rules."

"She's a rotten influence on you." Grandma appeared in the peony hallway.

"So hot." Dee blew on her tea.

Grandma Susannah flashed in front of Vianna, jaw clenched and eyes narrowed. "You will listen to me. Do not let *him* into this house again."

Grandma didn't like anyone non-witch in the house, so Vianna didn't put much stock into her warnings. Walking through her ghost sent a wave of flesh bumps over her arms. She headed down the hall and took a good look at the flooded bathroom and broken sink.

"With the Roots mantle fully descended, it is your *responsibility* to keep the house in check." Grandma floated behind her.

"I'm gonna have to make a trip to the hardware store. I guess we need sink handles." She picked up some of the wet towels. "And Ophelia stopped by."

"Oh?" Dee's voice rose in pitch.

"She mentioned something about a booth at the market?" Vianna purposely played coy, dragging out the inevitable planning storm that would take over Dee.

"She probably didn't have any? I knew it was a long shot, but it's impossible to even walk in the den anymore, there's so many candles and soaps from your late-night wanderings. Can you imagine how much you would have made?" Dee sighed dramatically. "We're still going though. *All* types of witches are allowed at the market. It's one of my favorite events."

"Well, your favorite event just got more hectic because Ophelia gave us a booth."

Dee spilled tea onto her hands as she bounced on the balls of her feet and squealed. "Oh, oh, oh. I knew it! Let me make a list. We need stuff for our booth."

A half hour later, and with a list that was longer than her arm, Vianna pulled into the parking lot of Hurley's Hardware. She found a spot near the front and headed in.

The overhead lights buzzed, and the linoleum peeled up around the metal shelving that formed rows in the middle of the store. It wasn't the nicest place, but Hurley had owned it for forever, and she much preferred small local shops to big chain stores.

Three aisles and two polite passes on help from the college kid in a neon vest at the checkout stand later, she found the bathroom sink section. The packages hanging on the display board looked more like something to fix a spaceship than a sink. She peeked back down the aisle at the college kid. Maybe he knew more about spaceships than she did.

"Vie?"

She twirled around to the familiar scent of canned bacon. It'd been awhile since she smelled that. Two pasty-white guys and a girl, all dressed in black grunge, stared at her from the other side of the aisle. She recognized the tallest of the three. James. He was the bacon smell. Memories from Boston and the cockroach-infested single bedroom she'd rented from his uncle flashed into her mind.

James had been an annoyance, the creepster who found every excuse possible to end up on her doorstep. He'd notoriously fixed every appliance in her place that wasn't broken to begin with.

He walked down the aisle toward her with the same greasy hair that hung in his eyes. The guy beside him sported a tossed shag that went to his ears and wore a sleeveless shirt that highlighted shoulders he clearly invested a lot of gym time into. The girl had a baseball cap with a ponytail hanging out the back and a backpack with stars slung over one shoulder. She held a basket filled with supplies that caught Vianna's attention. Chicken wire and solar panels were an odd combination.

"I was hoping we'd run into you." James's scuffed-up sneakers slapped against the linoleum as the other two strolled behind him. "I tried to hold on to your stuff when my uncle... well, you know." He stopped in front of her and gave a shrug.

"When he threw my crap out the second I came to Salem for my mother's funeral?" Vianna took a deep breath. What was done was done, and getting all riled about it again wouldn't help anything. "I remember."

James chewed on his thumbnail. "Yeah, not the first time he's been a dick."

"I'm Liam." Muscle Boy held out his arm for a handshake and winked.

"Oh, uh..." She looked at his hand but didn't shake it. She'd done nothing to give him the go-ahead for winking and inching into her space. "I'm Vianna."

James nudged between them. "I work with Liam, and that's his sister, Ruby. We have a gig here, actually." He sheepishly smiled up at her. "You might have heard of us. *Ghost Exposure.*"

Liam puffed up his chest, folding his arms and widening his stance like the paparazzi had just found him in the middle of a local hardware store. James straightened from his usual slouch, and the girl pulled her cap lower like she wanted to find a black hole to crawl into.

"Ghost Exposure?" Vianna focused back on James.

He pushed his hair from his face. "Paranormal investigators. I handle the filming. Ruby does the..." He stuttered a bit before coughing out, "Audio. And Liam is the host."

Vianna nodded. This had to be some kind of prank. Surely Dee was going to pop out from the other aisle any moment. Only, Dee wouldn't have involved pervy James. Dee didn't even know about James. So, not a prank, but a very good argument in Vianna's column for why *not* to go into paranormal investigating. There was no way these three actually interacted with ghosts, and Ruby's "audio" was likely setting up light illusions or using fishing line to move chairs.

For a moment, it felt too coincidental to run into someone she knew from Boston in the little Salem store, but Boston was just down the way, and if they were paranormal investigators, Salem was the biggest game in the area, only after the old Danvers State Hospital.

"You got a broken knob?" James pointed to the display of handles.

Liam snorted. Ruby sighed and left the aisle without a word.

"I can help fix that if you want." James looked down at her with hopeful eyes.

"I'm good." She gave a quick scan of sink handles and kits with twisting tubes and small plastic rings.

"Right. You were always that way." He grimaced.

She side-eyed him. *That way?* She wasn't touching that comment because she didn't need any more of whatever issues he had going on. Finding the exit sign for this awkward reunion was objective number one, which meant she needed to pick a handle—any handle at this point.

The wall of options all had two handles in the packaging. Apparently, she had to change both. She grabbed the kit with the most supplies because her rusted toolbox wasn't exactly a cornucopia of tools. Plus, it got bonus points for the biggest sale sign.

"Independent women are hot." Muscle Boy waggled his eyebrows from the other side of James.

She hugged the faucet kit against herself, making the plastic packaging dig into her arm. "Well, nice seeing you, James. Or something like that. Good luck with the filming." She rushed down the aisle.

"I'll text you," James hollered to her fleeting back. "We should catch up while I'm in town."

She waved a noncommittal hand in the air and turned the corner.

7

The Missing Bedazzler

On the drive back, Vianna tapped her rings against the steering wheel, chewing on thoughts of the past. Running into James had crashed her two worlds together. The Boston Vianna was a nobody, living in a rathole of an apartment with dreams of her own boutique to keep her afloat. The Salem Vianna was well-known by all the wrong people and had a home—even if demonic. But did she have any dreams? What kept her afloat?

In Salem, she was surrounded by a full garden and shelves filled with teas, lotions, and candles. Whether there was a shop or not, that fact would never change. But could she be a feared legacy witch and also own a boutique? There was no running away from being a witch, nor could she ignore the harm done by witches and by her own ancestors. The Boston Vianna had turned her back on all of that, but things were different now. When she'd run at sixteen, she couldn't have changed anything, couldn't have helped anyone—she could only survive. But now?

Paranormal investigating could give her the chance to find those who needed help, those trying to survive. And if the products sold at the witch market tonight, perhaps a boutique could still be a possibility too. Maybe she could be both Viannas, the one her heritage demanded and the one that gave her peace.

When she pulled into the driveway, once again someone was waiting. Mother had never had this many visitors when she was in charge. She'd get *maybe* one a year. Vianna felt like she had visitors at her door daily, hourly. She needed to work on her intimidation game.

A man lounged in a lawn chair beneath the tree in the front yard. The mohawk of locs tied into a fountain on top of his head was familiar. Csada. She couldn't think of a single reason for him to be here, but the unexpected visit did give her the opportunity to get more information about the mark in her yard, the mark that was directly beneath him. That couldn't be a coincidence.

Vianna opened the Jeep door and hopped out, crossing the lawn. Csada looked up at her through pink plastic sunglasses that matched the flamingos on his swim trunks. He was shoeless but wore a tattered cardigan that hung open, showing his scarred chest. The scars were intentional, made in shapes with a blade. She'd seen witches do the same in cutting tournaments. Vianna wrapped her arms around herself to shield against the autumn breeze that didn't seem to affect him.

"Hello, baby witch." He shimmied his backside further into the lawn chair that looked as bad as Vianna's rusted old backyard furniture. *Hold up.*

Her hands dropped to her hips. "That's *my* lawn chair."

"You should invest in something nicer. It's..." He shifted his shoulders. "Itchy."

The front door swung open, and Dee stomped onto the porch. "He's been here since right after you left."

"Did he sa—" Vianna looked toward the house and paused, staring at the colored fluffs drifting in the air. Vianna craned her neck to look around Dee and through the open door. A bomb of rainbow tulle had gone off in the house. It was the only explanation.

"No," Dee said, pulling Vianna's attention back. "He did not say why he is here."

"Mademoiselle Sandeen." Csada purred the 'e' in her name. "I invited you to join me for a sit." He patted on his lap.

"Nope." Dee rested a hand on her cocked hip and gave a fix-this-shit look to Vianna. "I would have gotten the hose, but I knew you had some questions."

She did, but instead he blurted a question first.

"The house has fewer occupants than my last visit. Yes? Why?"

Vianna narrowed her eyes at him. She'd gained a roommate since his last visit, equaling more occupants to the average eye, but there were *technically* fewer with the banished ghosts. It wasn't just Nancy gone, but Bathroom Earl and Uncle Jasper. Perhaps it was Csada's hoodoo background that made him more aware.

"Your math is off. There was one, and now there are two." Vianna gave her best effort at a stern poker face.

Csada raised a pierced brow and smirked. "Are you sure?"

A wet *thump* came from the rain gutters overhead. Csada's head flinched to the side as a putrid, brown lump slapped his cheek, then rolled down his chest, smearing mucus on his cream cardigan. Limp frog limbs splayed across his stomach.

Csada looked down, head tilted.

Vianna grinned. "That's Shuck's way of saying you should leave."

"Shuck," Csada repeated, letting the name linger on his tongue.

Shit. She scrunched her nose. Names mattered, and she'd just handed over a golden nugget.

"Perhaps it's a matter of perspective." Csada stood from the chair, the ball of rotting slime cupped in his hands. "What's a warning to another may be a gift to the *right* person."

"That's one hell of a sales gimmick." Dee snorted from the porch. "Turning a dead frog into some special gift."

Csada used a finger to play with a floppy frog leg. "It's all in your perspective. Like witches." His eyes tracked up to Vianna's, and his grin slid into a grim, thin line. "You are not mysterious creatures. You find strength in numbers, like swarms of insects on a rotting corpse, leaching magic from demons because you have none of your own."

Vianna resisted folding her arms over her chest. She was fidgety and uncomfortable, but he didn't need to know that. "Yet, here you are, uninvited and in the middle of witch territory. And marking my lawn, no less."

"You marked it for me, baby witch."

So it was a mark. But for what? "I told you I'm not selling the house. There's nothing here for you."

They stood there for a moment, Vianna glaring but unwilling to look away. Csada broke into a large, crooked smile, washing away the tension in the air. With a shrug, he turned and strolled away, taking the dead frog with him as he whistled a happy tune. Vianna let out a slow breath, watching him until he was out of sight.

"Hmmm." Dee clicked her nails, each one against her thumb, as she stared after him.

Vianna headed up the porch to join her. "Yeah. I don't like it either. Keep an eye out for anything. I'll ask Tuck for more details about him once he gets back into town and this ghost thing is handled."

Dee went inside the house, and Vianna followed, stopping just a few steps inside. It wasn't just rainbow tulle everywhere, but every craft known to mankind was strewn across the living room, into the kitchen, and even up the stairs. Strips of cut burlap and lace lay in piles on the couch, and the supplies from the candle den that had been overflowing from the shelves now littered every surface and most of the floor. The only open space to set the bags down on was on the bottom stair.

Dee kept walking once inside, veering past the piles and heading straight for the back door. Vianna followed, then gasped when she saw the pile of branches piled by the porch.

"My tree!" Over the past few months, Vianna had buried pouches of homemade remedies in the soil and smeared poultices over the bark to keep the tree from dying. Having a blackthorn die was bad luck that she didn't want to risk. All the effort had also made her a bit attached.

Dee hefted a stray branch from below the tree. "You need to breathe. I'm well-read on tree trimming, and you're too conservative with your pruning. Help me get this into the truck."

"You better be right." Vianna looked around the deck, taking in the rest of the mess. "Why do you need branches?"

"To hang tea bags and herbs from at the booth. We can tie the branches to the poles so it will look like our booth is in the forest." Dee dragged the branch to the pile, then counted them all, seeming satisfied with the results.

Vianna pointed to a wheelbarrow propped upside down with water dripping from it. "And that?"

"We can fill it with quartz and stagger candles within," Dee said. "As long as you grabbed that black spray paint from the hardware store?"

"Yeah," Vianna said, eyeing the wheelbarrow. They did have bags of clear quartz in the den. It was the base for every spelled candle and used to cleanse batches of herbs. Using it as decoration couldn't hurt anything. "I got everything but the bedazzler, which I assumed was a joke because you know Hurley doesn't stock those. You had to special-order your first one. Why do you need two, anyway?"

Dee thinned her lips into a grimace, then stepped over the branches to stomp up the porch stairs. "Because I can't find mine. It's gone missing, along with every teal thing I own. Which, by the way, is a lot of stuff because it's my favorite color. Tell your pet-house that he's not funny and I want my stuff back."

Vianna opened her mouth, then closed it, following Dee into the house. Wherever Shuck had hidden the bedazzler, it was for the better. When even the dish gloves were lined with rhinestones, it was a bit overboard.

Dee buzzed right through the kitchen, down the hall, and into the den. The aroma of cedar and allspice lingered in the air, but the shelves were almost bare. Dee had commandeered the back half of the room for potion making, and it was still ripe with goodies. She had a cauldron on the potbellied stove, and fingertips of white smoke reached over the lip. There was always something brewing in Dee's cauldrons.

Vianna tugged strands from a pile of hay on the edge of the shelf, twisting them into the beginnings of a Mabon doll out of habit. Dee pulled a wicker cornucopia from a top shelf and set it on the table, then perused drawers and shelves, snagging all sorts of leaves, dried nuts, and charms along the way. She piled everything onto the middle of the rectangular oak table and gave Vianna a huge grin.

"I thought this could be the base for our centerpiece." Dee's eyes were so wide with excitement she might as well have had stars in them. "For the booth tonight. It's the last part to plan. I was waiting for you."

"I see." Vianna raised a brow. She'd been to countless witch markets through the years, and the centerpieces were never just about decoration.

Dee moved around the room, gathering oils and dried flowers at random. An excited energy filled the air, and it wasn't just Dee; Shuck knew what they were up to as well. Centerpieces at the market were a symbol of protection from a witch's familiar. Sometimes they were merely a symbol to scare a thieving witch into thinking twice, but other times they were filled with nasty magic that would maim a witch to set an example. Since bluffing wasn't a common tactic among witches, more of the maiming happened than not.

Vianna tied off the doll of hay and tossed it onto the table. "I saw a witch try to steal from a booth once."

Dee slid a knee onto a stool, then sat on it. "You did not."

Vianna nodded, picking up an acorn and rolling it between her palms. "Mistress Epsler's booth."

"No," Dee gasped. "I thought that was a rumor."

"Oh, it really happened. I was little, probably around nine, but I'll never forget that scream. Everyone around her froze, and it was like time slowed as the crowds gawked. I didn't want to see it, tried hiding behind Mother, but she shoved me to the front and forced me to watch."

"Did a flock of birds really peck the thief to death—piece by piece—carrying the collection of flesh to the woods? That's what I heard." Dee leaned an elbow on the table, enthralled.

"Just the eyes." Vianna grimaced. "They were shadow birds, and every dark movement in the trees outside of my window made me jump for months." In truth, she still felt jumpy with shifting shadows. That was just common sense.

"Why the eyes?" Dee asked.

"She accused Epsler of having fake feathers. Said there was no way they were real. Epsler claimed that since the witch's eyes didn't work so well, she didn't have need for them." The memory of rage in a dirt-smudged Epsler's face as she stood over the offending witch was haunting.

Dee frowned, then sighed dramatically.

"What?" Vianna asked.

Dee clicked each nail against her thumb, her thinking tick. "Epsler is a solitary. And I'm guessing that was her first time at the markets, at least with a booth. She was being tested."

Dee didn't have to say the rest. It was likely tonight wouldn't go easy for them, not that Vianna had expected a cheerful greeting at any witch event. Zosia's threats at Charles's speech were a prime example. But if they were tested at the market and didn't hold their own, it was likely they'd be seen as easy targets for every initiation class of every coven for the next five generations, or more. Not to mention they'd never get another booth.

"Come on." Vianna grabbed Dee's wrist and tugged her out of the den. "We need better supplies."

Once they were in the hallway, the door to the conjure room slowly creaked open on its own. Shuck knew Vianna's intent. If she was entering a tangled nest of witches intent on testing her worth, wishful thinking and snappy comebacks wouldn't cut it. She needed magic.

The moment they walked through the door, the drawer with the Roots grimoire clicked open. Shuck was eager. Vianna crossed the room and used both hands to pull the heavy, tattered book from the desk.

"Did Angeline ever have a booth at the market?" Dee strolled along the shelves that lined each wall, inspecting everything.

"No." Vianna sat in the chair at the desk. "Mother never had products to sell. She was a service for hire, but only through the coven."

Vianna flipped through pages that were quickly becoming memorized. In the past few months, she'd spent just as much time with her nose in the grimoire as she had fiddling in the candle den or garden. She wouldn't carry on the legacy of murder that came with her last name, but that didn't mean she'd let herself be easy prey.

"Ya know, he stole my favorite pair of strappy wedges. The ones with crystals in the hemp." Dee picked up a jar of dung beetles caught in honey, tipping it upside down and looking closer.

"Focus, Dee," Vianna said. "We need his help for a legit centerpiece."

"The centerpieces aren't just about protection talismans or standard spells. They're a show of power unique to that demon. Epsler is bound to some intense crow-demon if the rumors are true."

Vianna paused from flipping pages, giving Dee her full attention.

"So we can't do just anything," Dee said. "It has to be something where Shuck gets to come out and play."

"I don't know," Vianna said. "Shuck's idea of playtime likely involves bodies."

"Hold up. Let's not go straight to doom and gloom. There's more to him, ya know, like his affinity for sparkle and teal. The little klepto." Dee set the honey-beetle jar back on the shelf.

Vianna drummed her fingers against the open grimoire as an idea formed. "What if we give him other pockets to pick?"

"I'm listening." Dee turned toward Vianna with a hand on her hip.

"The grimoire doesn't have a spell about how to turn your familiar into a pickpocket. Well, not that exactly, but there is an echo spell." Vianna began to flip pages to find the spell.

"An echo?" Dee repeated.

"Yeah," Vianna said. "It sends out a signal to find something. What if we reversed it? The tracked object would be stolen goods from the booth. If someone tries to take something without fair trade, they create a connection that allows Shuck access to their pockets."

Dee turned toward Vianna, brow raised. "Oh, that could work. It's like demon echolocation."

"Exactly." Vianna picked up the grimoire and crossed to the drawers lining the far wall. "I don't know how far of a distance he'll be able to track the target, but we can try."

Balancing the leather book on her hip, she used her other hand to open drawers, collecting dried reishi mushrooms, red dianthus petals, and a black envelope with a sketch of a cat on the front. Dee gathered black and red candles, lighting them in the four directional points of the circle carved into the floor of the room.

"A star of anise with rosemary oil drops on the candle, patchouli incense, and an ostrich feather." Vianna listed ingredients for the echo spell they were using as a base.

"On it." Dee moved to the shelves on the other side of the room. She'd spent her fair share of time in the conjure room and moved straight to the corner where the feathers were kept. Vianna had insisted Dee was welcome to browse the conjure room and use whatever she needed for potion making. So far, Dee was adding to the collection more than using it.

"An ostrich feather represents truth," Dee said. "Maybe a wren instead? For safe travel."

Vianna unpinned a dead tiger beetle from an entomology board. "I like it."

After piling their loot in the middle of the circle, they both sat cross-legged, facing each other with the grimoire between them. Dee lit incense in an abalone shell, along with a candle in the center of the circle, as Vianna measured out ingredients.

"The chant calls to something lost returning home. We'll have to scrap the whole thing and make our own." Vianna crushed the ingredients into the mortar with the pestle as she eyed the grimoire.

"Oh, we're fan-tabulous at that." Dee gave a grin. "The klepto-echo spell." She made an 'O' with her lips. "That's a good name. So it's not so much a call but an invitation, right?"

"A wrong to be righted, an invitation sent." Vianna mashed the last chunks in the paste and set the mortar on the floor between her and the grimoire. "A thief's pockets unbound."

"Oooh, I like that," Dee said.

Vianna smeared the paste into the indents of the star of anise, then slid it into the wet wax of a lit candle.

"Loot pilfered..." Vianna let the words linger on her lips as she thought. The flame from the candle stretched higher. The connection to Shuck warmed within her chest, feeling heavy. "A thief's pockets unbound. With something taken, an opportunity given, an invitation for the hellhound."

A loud pop shook the floorboards, and for a brief moment, black shimmers bounced in the air. And then nothing.

"That never gets old," Dee whispered. Her eyes were downcast, staring at the candle.

They'd done numerous spells together over the months, but with only two of them, it was spell work for one. Dee's potions were potent and spectacular, but she couldn't spell the ingredients needed for them to work. Vianna had to do that part. It took three witches to work coven spells; two wasn't enough, making Dee an observer only.

"Come on." Vianna plucked the star from the candle and held it up. "Let's go add this to your cornucopia. No one will notice it among all the other goodies you've got."

Dee brightened. "I found the best rust-colored glitter. It's going to look amaze-balls."

Was it too much to hope that glitter was next on Shuck's list of items to go missing?

A vibration shook within Vianna's chest, followed immediately by a knock at the front door. Both Vianna and Dee straightened, looking at each other with pinched expressions.

"I don't suppose Shuck is using words yet? Maybe give us a little insight on whether we can ignore the door or if we need to bring a weapon." Dee stood up with a sigh. "There's no in-between."

Vianna stood up too. "I suppose a weapon never hurts."

"That's not exactly encouraging," Dee mumbled as she followed Vianna.

When Vianna opened the door, she scrunched her face in confusion. "James?"

8

The Loggerhead Sea Turtle

James shuffled from one worn tennis shoe to the other, his pants covered in pockets with weird shapes poking out. The smell of canned bacon permeated from him. Liam, the muscle-bound, ghost-hunting buddy, leaned against her porch railing behind him. His sister Ruby wore a large hoodie instead of the baseball cap.

"Hey, Vie." James pushed hair from his eyes.

"What are you doing here?" Vianna blurted.

Dee opened the door the rest of the way, taking in their visitors as she stepped beside Vianna. Grandma appeared at her other side, arms crossed over her noose.

"Dee," Vianna said. "This is James Hughes. His uncle was my landlord in Boston."

"I remember him," Dee said. "The *Jeopardy* asshole who threw out your stuff."

James's brow shot up, and he shook his head. "My uncle is a total jerk. I'm not like him."

He might not be like his uncle, but he gave off his own special brand of the heebie-jeebies. In Boston, Vianna had felt like he lurked around every corner, doing who-knew-what.

Muscle Boy stepped forward and introduced himself to Dee. "I'm Liam, host of *Ghost Exposure*. We're ghost hunters. You might have already heard of us."

Dee did a slow head turn toward Vianna. Amusement lit her eyes. "Ghost hunters. How intriguing."

"We're legit." Liam lifted his chin. "Not some rinky-dink home-made production or whatever you're thinking. We were *invited* to Salem."

Dee nodded with thinned lips. She looked as doubtful as Vianna felt. Businesses needing a boost of exposure often called in shows like that, so maybe they had been invited, but not for the legitimacy Liam seemed to imply.

James shoved him aside. "I told you I got this. I know her."

"Bro, *I* got this. Where's your camera? It's, like, your only job." Liam focused back on Vianna and Dee, his large smile as fake as a Ken doll. "James says you've lived in Salem your whole life?"

Despite the pinched expression on James's face, he did what Liam said and turned on the camera.

The blinking red light that signaled filming transformed Liam from a bro into someone relaxed and confident. "Could you give us an insider view of Salem, the most haunted town in America? What kind of stuff have you seen? You know, the *real* stuff."

"Do you really think you can just stroll up to someone's private residence and start recording them?" Dee stared down James, and he lowered the camera.

"How did you even get my address?" Vianna asked.

Ruby snorted. "Google. You popped right up."

Google. That made sense. Sometimes Vianna forgot that there was a whole world of people out there who weren't witches follow-ing some secret protocol for engaging with one another. Vianna being a legacy witch wasn't something these three would under-stand. To them, she was just Boston Vianna.

"What is a Google? Is this child ogling you?" Grandma circled Ruby. "She is grossly inappropriate."

"I can feel your energy. You're like me." Liam's expression soft-ened, and a slight frown pulled at his lips. Vianna really hoped he didn't actually think this was gonna work.

"Who is this dalcop and his barnacles?" Grandma shifted her attention to Liam.

"Your parents died too, didn't they?" Liam was doing serious sad eyes, all wide and empty.

Grandma straightened, assessing him. "Is he looking to hire for a job? Charge him double. He doesn't know one eternity box from another."

"Yeah, yeah, yeah. You can Google. We know." Dee was pushing his buttons and Vianna would bet money it was on purpose.

"No." Liam's face went rigid, and his shoulders pulled back as he straightened. "I didn't Google her. I can feel her energy."

Vianna was over this song and dance. They had to finish prep for the market. The sun was slipping behind the horizon, and it was almost time to head out. "I can't help you guys. I don't have any ghost stories." At least, none that she wanted to share.

"Vie." James stacked his equipment by the railing. "Hold up. Can we talk?" He motioned with his chin to the other end of the porch.

"I really don't have any stories for you. Maybe whoever hired you will have some local tour guides or something. They're trained to keep an ear out for that kind of stuff." She hugged herself against a slight breeze that rustled her hair.

"For old times' sake? Please." James did a full-on bottom lip pout.

There weren't any old times between them, unless he counted her avoidance tactics that he always seemed to outsmart. But letting him speak his piece seemed like the best way to get him to leave.

With a sigh, she followed him to the other end of the wraparound porch. The floorboards creaked with every step, making it clear that Shuck was not impressed.

"Vianna." A bright red spread over James's cheeks. "I—I, well... I'm a little nervous."

He rubbed his hands together, then blew a deep breath into his cupped palms. He rocked from his heels to his toes. This wasn't good. Every possible reason for James to be red-faced around her were scenarios she wanted nothing to do with.

"I... kinda watched you in Boston." James's eyes darted to the shrubs around the porch instead of making eye contact. "I know you can see ghosts. For real."

Vianna's gut tightened. She felt like she'd been whacked with a bat.

"At first, I just thought you were a little off, like maybe you had some medication you'd stopped taking, and I felt sorry for you." He scrunched his face in a constipated-concern expression.

She grimaced. He was outing her and insulting her all in one swoop. He stepped closer. Vianna stepped backward, and the porch railing post hit her lower back.

James blurted more words in a rush. "So then I started offering to help around the apartment, and you were always so jumpy, your eyes darting this way and that. Something didn't add up, so I started watching you. And it was easier than I expected. With how you always left blinds open and stuck to the same schedule, it just all kinda fell into place, like it was meant to be. And it was."

Vianna went still, focusing on breathing in and out. They weren't alone, and he was on her home turf. She was the scary one in this scenario—or at least, she should be.

James was still rattling on. "It wasn't until I realized you avoided the same spot in the elevator. You always stood scrunched into the right corner like something was going to get you. And then I remembered the murder that happened right before you moved in. It all became so obvious. You could see the ghost."

That didn't feel obvious to her. "James." Vianna held up her hands for him to stop. "I don't know what you're talking about." She did, but it wasn't any of his business.

"It's okay." James smiled. "You don't have to hide things from me. It's a lot to digest, but I found this group of people. Not just Liam and Ruby, but others, and it's okay that you're weird. It's okay that I'm weird. I can help you have a normal life, because 'normal' *isn't* normal. You'll fit in with us. No, not just fit in—you'll be like a rockstar with your abilities. We'll all be famous after that."

Vianna shook her head. "You have the wrong person." His jumbled nonsense spun in her head, but she kept circling back to the same thing. He knew. He knew she could see ghosts, and he could tell just by watching her. "You need to leave. I'm not interested in your people. I have my own, and you're very confused about who I am."

James nodded, as though Vianna had asked him a question. His eyes somehow looked larger, pleading. "It's a lot. Think about it."

He turned and nodded to Liam. "Maybe we should go. I have another name I found online that we can hit up for backstory. Vianna just needs some time to think."

"No, I don't, James," Vianna said to his back.

James didn't acknowledge her, just kept walking, down the porch and off the property. His ghost team followed behind.

Dee leaned into Vianna with her voice lowered. "Why do you seem spooked? Those guys were goobers."

"James accused me of being able to see ghosts. Wanted me to... help his show, I think."

"Huh," Dee said.

They turned and went back into the house. "You don't seem all that surprised."

"Yes and no." Dee began to load a pile of products into a storage bin. "It's not the world's biggest mystery, but he didn't seem that observant to me either, so it's a little surprising."

It wasn't the first time Dee had mentioned how shifty Vianna could look sometimes, so maybe it really wasn't the biggest leap for someone who knew what they were looking for. "Can you let me know next time I go all ghost-shifty or whatever? Maybe I can work on it."

"Sure." Dee didn't look up, but kept loading the Tupperware as though it were perfectly normal to ask for help with facial expressions.

Vianna grabbed another bin and began to load another pile. "Thanks. For helping." They had the booth thanks to her, too. "And for everything."

Dee paused, then bumped shoulders with Vianna. "Anytime. Maybe one day your first assumption in any situation will be that I have your back. Because I do."

"I know." She tucked in a pack of rose-and-eucalyptus bath tea into the corner of the bin. "It's new. I'll get better at this. I really am grateful for you."

"Obviously." Dee snapped on the lid to her bin. "I'm awesome."

Vianna chuckled. "It's true."

A few hours later and they were loaded and driving to the docks in Vianna's old Ford. The sun was setting but still too bright, not quite that soothing Creamsicle phase. She thrummed her fingers against the cracked plastic of the steering wheel, each ring—including the red cinnabar talisman—clicking in an even pattern. She had slipped on the ring as a last-minute decision, which meant Grandma Susannah and Clarice were invited along for the festivities. Grandma might be outdated, uncouth, and a pain in the ass, but she'd likely see an attack coming before anyone else. And what Grandma Susannah didn't see coming, Grandma Clarice would.

Both grandmas sat between Vianna and Dee in the middle of the bucket seat. It took effort not to flinch at the stray beetles getting too close. Dee reached through both grandmas, handing Vianna a PB&J sandwich. She'd packed dinner to go so they wouldn't be late. Dee was never on time, much less early to anything, except the witch market, it seemed.

"Proper witches wear proper robes to the Mabon bonfire," Grandma repeated for the billionth time.

Vianna would not let Grandma under her skin. Especially since she'd dressed up more than usual with crisp black jeans, a nice fluffy sweater, and strappy boots. She'd thought she looked nice, but anything other than ceremonial robes wasn't worth mentioning around Grandma. Dee wore a dark layered wrap dress that seemed to have the proper vibe since Grandma didn't comment on her outfit.

"So." Dee's voice broke Vianna's thoughts. "What are you going to do about James?"

She turned off the main road, toward the docks. "I don't know. Think I can just ignore it until he goes away?"

Dee snorted.

Yeah, she'd kinda figured that. "No one has ever just come out and guessed my ghost-seeing ability before."

"Why is that, anyway?" Dee asked. "Why *him* of all people?"

"I was thinking about that. My apartment was basically a roach motel, and there were a lot of death loops, almost as many as a cemetery or hospital. I hated it there. I probably looked like a walking freak show."

The passenger front side of the truck dipped with a clank, then bounced back onto the road. Dee smashed against the window and both of the grandmas levitated a foot into the air.

"Holy driving issues," Dee huffed. "I think you just dropped a piece of this ancient dinosaur back there."

"Hey." Vianna frowned. "This dinosaur is indestructible."

"Ugh." Dee dragged out the last syllable. "I hate not driving."

Vianna braked before turning right toward the ocean. She slowed the truck for the predictable crew blocking the road. They all wore wide-brim hats or sun visors with matching shirts that read 'Slow down for the Loggerhead Sea Turtle'. Every year they chose a different endangered species, beach cleanup, or some other excuse to close the area off. The excuse was construction when Vianna was younger, but tourists hadn't respected those boundaries the last few years, so the covens had switched tactics.

The truck slowed to a stop, and a broad-shouldered, turtle-loving man approached. He had a wide-brim fishing cap and coiled wire in his ear. "Qualifications, ma'am."

Vianna pulled her sweater down, exposing the marking on her collarbone, and the man snapped a picture with his phone. After a few moments, he nodded at Dee. "And you?"

Dee held out her phone, showing a photo of a caramel-colored stone with red swirls. For witches without a coven or demon markings, a particular stone was chosen as a password for each event. The man nodded and waved them in.

When they drove through the invisible ward surrounding the market, a ripple of shivers ran between Vianna's shoulders, making her feel like a lit-up sparkler.

Dee rubbed her hands together. "Feels like magic."

"Yes, it does," Vianna agreed. With just the right amount of fear mixed in.

9

The Witch Market

Vianna pulled into a spot between a rented U-Haul and a compact, red Volkswagen in the back of a nearly full parking lot. They unloaded the portable moving dolly with a large metal bed, snapping the handle into place before loading a towering pile of large Tupperware and branches propped up between. Mother had used the dollies for handling sacrifices—animal and *other*—so moving decorations was a nice change.

It took both of them to push the over packed dolly past the displays being set up for other booths. Both grandmas followed behind them. Vianna suddenly felt four feet tall again, flashing back to walking this same shore as a kid, the racks of dried chicken claws, the salted breeze catching in tinkling bells, and the air filled with the aroma of every herb known to man. The same ghosts lingered too. A man collapsed to his knees in the rocks with a hand on his chest. A woman was dragged by her hair into the shallow waters below the dock. Vianna shook off the ache in her chest. She wasn't here for the dead. She would focus instead on the living.

Booths stretched along the shore and spilled onto the dock. Mistress Epsler and her birds were positioned where the dock ended and the beach began. The dead fowl hung in tiers of bright fuchsia, tangerine, sunbeam, and Caribbean blue, acting as borders from the booth's neighbors. Espler's birds were a fashion trend that every witch bought into. She raised them on spelled food, giving the feathers their extra-vibrant hues and, rumors claimed, a stronger magical kick. Witches paid per feather and plucked their own.

Next to Epsler was Mistress Kanker with her scorpions. She sold stingers, blood vials, dried blood flakes, crushed legs, all parts of the scorpion—in all sizes. The largest of her collection sat in the center of a tall table. It was as thick as Vianna's thigh, with black lights that highlighted its every twitch. It didn't take much of an imagination to figure out what would happen if someone stole from Mistress Kanker. She was a member of the Lunar Coven and the scorpion was her familiar.

Other booths boasted specialty teas that didn't cure ailments but brought them on: stones pulled from the innards of exotic animals, goat breeders with docile sacrifices, black market human organs, and even a hoaxy demon whisperer that only Google witches would fall for.

Their booth placement was surprisingly decent: on the dock and primed for snagging Tidal witches as they disembarked from their ships with goodies from their looting. Vianna tucked the nagging thought of what Ophelia had gained from giving up this booth—in this cherry spot—to the back of her mind. She'd chew on that later. They were in the middle of the dock, sandwiched between two Lunar Coven witches, one selling a variety of night-blooming bulbs that Vianna had every intention of perusing, and the other selling custom tarot cards with matching crystals.

"It's a slight not to be positioned among your own coven." Grandma Susannah's upper lip twitched. It didn't matter how many times Vianna told Grandma she wasn't joining the OBC; her mind was set. Grandma Clarice wandered further down, distracted by a booth filled with jars of live insects and entomology boards dissecting the larger ones.

Dee turned into a whirlwind of action, somehow transforming the broken canopy she'd found in the corner of Vianna's gardening shed into a functional framework for their booth. She hung swaths of fabric in varying colors and textures to create an awning and set glittering gemstones along with the quartz in the wheelbarrow to showcase their wares. There wasn't another booth that sported shimmering fabrics or gemstones, and that felt appropriate. They belonged but didn't fit. It was their brand.

Vianna was unloading the last box of vanilla-sage candles when a sheet of fog slid over her feet. Dee paused from hanging tea bags from the hawthorn branches tied to the metal frame, eyes wide with the same excitement Vianna felt. Her heart thumped faster, and she stepped from the booth. Every witch along the dock and shoreline— including the grandmas—stopped their bustling to watch the same fog-coated horizon. The Tidal Coven would soon be in the harbor.

A wooden foremast of an old pirate ship broke through first. Gray sails fluttered in the breeze and a kraken was carved into the tip of the bow, tentacles reaching behind and over the ship. Everyone knew of the *Diamond*. There was no faster ship nor one more covered in magic. After that was a yacht, tall and shiny with what looked like a sorority party in full swing on its deck. A beast of a fishing vessel and a converted rescue water boat tugged into the opening at the same time. The last was a petite, lurking battleship. Five family lines captained ships, and the rest of their coven filled other roles aboard each.

As the ships moved closer, Anastasia Hall, the Tidal Coven mother, strolled down the dock. Soft layers of chemise billowed around her brown boots as she stretched out her arms, greeting her fleet. The ships docked and Tidal witches poured from their bows, funneling onto the main dock where the market began.

Everyone broke into action, bartering, squabbling, hauling large sacks and crates from ships, and younger witches running up and down the dock frantically. Every booth quickly filled to capacity with haggling witches, some with coven markings, some with familiars perched on their shoulder or trailing their steps, and a few Google witches trying to look like they belonged—the wide eyes and open mouths gave them away every time.

"Your booth looks like unicorn vomit. Smells like it too."

Vianna turned to see Tiphonie in a silken black dress that was more like lingerie than something to wear in public. Her red lipstick matched her silken hair. The Ramsey twins lingered behind her, as usual, one of them frowning as she glanced at the wheelbarrow of candles. Her normally long curls were chopped into a pixie cut, probably because they'd caught fire when they tried to burn down Vianna's house. Consequences were a snatch like that. A fourth witch with braided buns broke from their group, slipping deeper into the booth, examining products. Vianna wasn't sure if Bun Head was with Tiphonie or not.

"This one again? She ought to be taught a lesson." Grandma Susannah stepped in front of Vianna, raising her chin at Tiphonie. "It would be a good show for your coven to remember your worth. Release Shuck. Now. He'll guide you."

Yeah, that wasn't happening—it was exactly what Vianna was trying to avoid. As effective as mutilation and torture were, there were other ways to go about things.

"It seems unicorn vomit makes a good profit. I know I'd pay handsomely for it." Dee walked over, giving Tiph a wink.

"Tell your guard dog to heel." Tiphonie flicked a red curl over her shoulder. "You and this bawdy booth are a disgrace. You don't belong here."

"Bawdy?" Vianna puckered her lips, rolling the word over in her head. "Like sexually comical?"

There was a trio of Mabon witches browsing teas, and one of them gave a snort. Tiphonie's neck and cheeks colored, but it didn't stop her from scowling at Vianna as though it were her fault.

The pixie-cut twin sighed dramatically. "Gaudy. She meant your booth is garish and ugly."

"There are plenty of other booths," Vianna said. "Why don't you do us both a favor and move on?"

"I'm sure she'll find whatever *bawdy* trinkets she's looking for elsewhere." The lilt in Dee's voice made it hard not to grin.

Tiphonie crinkled her too-tiny nose. "I'm here for coven business. Not to buy your cheap junk." She smoothed the front of her slip dress with both hands. "You need to attend the next coven meeting in order to properly decline your coven status."

"What?" Grandma screeched. "Stitch her blasphemous lips closed so she won't spread her filth."

Grandma's reaction was predictable, but Tiphonie's request was a surprise. Vianna considered pointing out that climbing from her window and running away ten years ago seemed as official of a decline as it went. Truth be told, Vianna wasn't entirely sure what the proper way to decline the Original Blood Coven was. At least, not while keeping her heart beating at the same time.

"A coven mother is needed to sever a legacy line." Dee sidestepped two older witches wearing matching pumpkin-colored crocheted shawls and sorting through a pile of orange zest fire starters. "And rumor has it, the coven's divided on who should be the next mother."

"No one asked you." Tiph rolled her eyes.

"Rumor has it," Dee continued. "You're in the running, but the older matrons think you're too young. Wait, that wasn't the word they used. Hmmm." Dee tapped her long confetti nails against the side of her mouth. "Ah! *Immature.* That's what it was. Your only hope is to bag Charles. How's that playing out, by the way? I don't see a ring on that finger."

"Shut your trap," Tiphonie barked, making a few witches glance over. She lowered her voice. "In two full moons, the coven is voting, and my first line of business will be taking out the trash. Make it easy for both of us and officially decline before then."

Tiph nudged the table with her hip as she turned and strolled off, knocking a candle to the wooden slats below. Glass shattered. "And leave the wannabe witch at home."

The trio left, quickly engulfed in the bustling crowd. Vianna wanted to chuck a rock at their heads. Grandma clucked her tongue and turned away. With a deep breath, Vianna knelt down to clean up the mess.

She spoke to Dee as she cleaned. "They're assholes in general, but it's different with you. You're a lit-up neon target for them—every time. It makes me irate." Vianna put broken pieces into a bag that Dee held out for her. "Makes me want to hurt them," she whispered, keeping her eyes on the smaller glass shards as she gathered them with shaking fingers.

"I do not wear neon." Dee grinned. "Anyway, it says more about them than me. Witches who go for the easiest target are too weak to be worth caring about. Like gnats. Annoying, but ineffective in anything that really matters. I'm not letting them affect my day." Dee held out a hand to help Vianna up. "But I like that you care and get all protective. Ooh... how about Poltergeist Punishers?" Dee shook her head. "No. Never mind. I don't like the sound of it."

A sharp pain sliced beneath Vianna's collarbone, then through her shoulder. She flinched just as a low rumble shook the dock, making every witch stumble. A scream came from the dock, and both Vianna and Dee straightened, eyes wide. A crowd of both young and old swarmed, quickly blocking Vianna from seeing what was happening.

A screech tore from the crowd. "My hand!"

Vianna's blood went cold. She pushed through some younger witches who smelled of tobacco and wore cocktail dresses with combat boots. Lying on the deck was the witch with braided buns, holding her hand to her chest and soaking her yellow satin blouse with crimson. Tiphonie and the Ramsey twins were nowhere to be seen.

"She's a new OBC initiate," a witch whispered to her friend beside Vianna. "Did she steal from a booth? Was it a familiar attack?"

"Look," the friend said. "There's a broken candle by her. It's from the Roots booth."

"Holy goddess. No way."

The gossiping duo didn't seem to have a clue who Vianna was because they didn't give her a second thought, glancing back at the booth where Dee still stood, arms crossed and looking to Vianna for answers. Vianna pushed closer, and, sure enough, one of her candles was shattered against the dock. *Rotten goat balls.*

She didn't want to look but couldn't stop herself, stepping closer to the fallen witch. The crowd hushed. The girl held up her hand at Vianna. The last two fingers were missing, and a torn piece of flesh hung down her palm. Giving Shuck free rein to steal body parts had not been part of the plan. He was supposed to steal other products in return, but clearly the spell hadn't been that specific.

Another growl shook the dock, and several witches from the crowd gasped. Shuck was making a statement, and all eyes were focused on her. Vianna counted breaths, in and out, gathering her thoughts and figuring out what to say. The woman had stolen from the booth. Shuck held to the responsibility he was charged with. Were the fingers going to show up in the house now? In the booth? Vianna cringed, glancing around the girl but seeing no spare digits.

"How could you?" the now eight-fingered witch yelled.

Vianna straightened, frustrated. She wasn't the one who had

stolen from a demon-bound witch at the market. That had been moronic. What sort of idiot did that? Whatever the Ramsey twins had told her, promised her, it hadn't been worth it. Vianna was sure they were behind this. Possibly Tiphonie too.

Looking around, Vianna narrowed her eyes at a pair of witches in white cardigans and Mary-Jane pumps. She pointed at them. "You two. Bandage her hand and take her to Zosia Ramsey." It'd been Zosia's daughters who caused this mess. She could deal with it.

Vianna took in the rest of the crowd. "And no one else steal from my damn booth." The last thing she needed was Shuck collecting more body parts.

Dee looped arms with her, tugging her away from the crowd as the cardigan girls rushed to help the downed witch. "Best witch market ever," Dee whispered.

They broke free of the crowd, and Vianna noticed a group of women standing a few feet away in the middle of the dock, all with amused expressions. Leave it to witches to find blood and gore amusing. There was a wide berth around the group as the onlookers gave them space. Upon closer look, Vianna realized one of the women was Ophelia, in a deep plum dress. She locked eyes with Vianna, and the group approached.

"Vianna Roots, this is Frankie Ashton." Ophelia gestured toward a tall woman with deep brown skin, sharp features, and full lips, who stood in the middle of the group.

"Ashton," Dee whispered.

Every witch knew of the Ashtons. They were one of the oldest lines in the Tidal Coven, and they owned the most revered ship, the one that looked like the pirate ships of old: the *Diamond*. There were countless tales of the strongest and bravest walking her plank, never to be seen again.

Frankie stepped forward, eyes on Vianna. "Just who I was looking for."

Fire Magic

For a single breath of a moment, time went still. The bustling noises of the market faded in Vianna's head, and the connection to Shuck exploded with tingles that spread over every inch of her skin, coating her in magic. It felt as though an unseen tendril of energy reached from Vianna toward Frankie, and she wondered if it was one familiar greeting another. There were a lot of things she still didn't know about familiars, or even Shuck. Either way, Vianna was confused by the seemingly deeper reaction to Frankie.

"She's been to the house." Grandma sneered at the woman. "Some hubble-bubble about missing familiars. Familiars do not go missing."

Vianna stood silently, digesting that information. Frankie Ashton had known her mother, and not just by name. She'd been to the Roots house. Grandma Clarice hovered close by, but she seemed more concerned with the blood mark on the dock from the witch who'd lost her finger than anything Vianna was doing. The rest of the crowd had dispersed, avoiding upsetting one of the revered

Tidal captains, but they still stole glances, undoubtedly in hopes of seeing something to gossip about.

"You look like a Roots, that's for sure." For some unknown reason, her own observation seemed to amuse Frankie, and she grinned.

Whatever history this woman had with the Roots witches, Vianna wanted to be clear that she wasn't the same as those before her. "I can assure you the similarities stop there."

Frankie tilted her head to the side, and a few of her long, thick locs slipped over her shoulder. "Interesting. Your mother was one of the most powerful witches I knew. I hope for your sake that there are a few more similarities."

It wasn't an insult, and from a legacy witch's perspective, she had a point. Only the strong survived in this world. But Vianna didn't want the kind of strength that came from cruelty; she still held out hope that she could survive this world and not be her mother. "I suppose time will tell."

Frankie nodded. "Indeed."

A mini-me of Frankie stepped from behind her with pigtail poofs and the same deep green eyes. If the Ashtons had a look, it was the eyes. Vianna didn't have a lot of experience with kids, and the difference between a seven-year-old and a ten-year-old was beyond her, but she looked to be in that age group.

"I'm Taylor Ashton. And one day it will be *my* job to care for the best ship on the seas." The little girl had a stern expression and a hand on her hip.

Legacies worked like that. Sometimes it was a sentient house passed down, and sometimes it was the most coveted pirate ship in all of history.

Dee lowered to the little girl's level. "I'm Sandeen Layton, but you can call me Dee."

The little girl grinned. "You can call me Taye."

Dee nodded in approval. "A pleasure to meet you, Taye, future captain of the *Diamond*."

"Layton..." The little girl pursed her lips, looking up at her mother. "Original Blood Coven?"

Frankie nodded. "That's correct."

History of the original covens was important to legacy witches. Memories flooded Vianna's mind, sitting at the kitchen table with parchment and pen, writing out family trees of all the legacy lines that Mother deemed important. The Ashton line had been a staple for the Tidal Coven.

"Ophelia mentioned we have a mutual acquaintance." Frankie strolled past them and into Vianna and Dee's booth. She walked along the back display, picked up a pumpkin-and-cedar-scented Mabon candle, then gave it a whiff. "Csada Laguerre has been snooping around your property?"

Ophelia took her cue and scooped up the little girl's hand in hers. "Come. I've heard of a special squid ink that glows in the dark. All the younger witches are getting tattoos with it. I want to see."

"That's Blake! She does all the ink. Can I show her, Mama?"

"Go ahead." Frankie nodded and glanced at the other woman with them. "I'll be right there."

"On it." The other woman trailed Ophelia and Taylor.

Frankie perused the booth, with Grandma hot on her heels, looking at the displays. Vianna and Dee stood in the middle, watching. The booth had cleared out of everyone but the three of them.

"I knew Csada when he was younger, and he's not what he seems." Frankie spun on her heel, facing them. "Whatever you've done to catch his attention, undo it."

Keeping Csada at a distance seemed as obvious as planting toward the east. "He wanted to buy the house, and that's obviously not happening."

"He marked your property?" Frankie went back to perusing, her fingers fluttering between tea bags.

She was referring to the marking from the war water. That's why Ophelia had arranged this happenstance meeting. "Yes. And he's all dodgy when asked about it."

"He's a collector of rare things." The creases around Frankie's eyes deepened. "Including familiars. Be careful."

Collecting familiars. Vianna stilled, coldness seeping through her as her breaths became shallow enough to be confused with the dead. Dee nudged an elbow into Vianna's ribs, and she sucked in air. Breathing was important. There would be no collecting Shuck, not by Rose and her brain-warped, first-generation beliefs and certainly not by some outcast hoodoo practitioner.

"How do I get rid of him?" Vianna growled, or maybe it was Shuck who growled within her chest. At least they were on the same page on this one.

"I don't know," Frankie answered.

Vianna narrowed her eyes. The infamous ship captain had come to offer a warning but no tips on how to handle it. *Helpful.* "Any other advice beyond 'undo it'?"

"You *are* a spunky thing." Frankie arched a brow. "Dealing with Csada comes at a cost. He's dangerous. So whatever you do, expect the unexpected."

As annoying as it was to get no advice other than to be careful, it doubled down on the impression Vianna already had on the situation. Csada was not to be trusted, and he wasn't just a nuisance ruining the grass in her front yard. He was a threat.

"The warning is appreciated." There was proper conduct for an information exchange between the older lines, and Vianna understood it well. It was the same formalities and the same vagueness as dealing with Mother. "If there's something I can assist you with, I'd be amicable. And perhaps you'll find more thoughts on how to deal with such a threat."

"Perhaps. Time will tell, right?" Frankie winked. "It was intriguing to meet you, Vianna." Not waiting for a reply, she left the booth and slipped into the crowds.

Dee stood beside Vianna. "Not exactly the answers we need."

Vianna nodded in agreement, but before she could reply, new faces, likely as curious about the dockside maiming as the glitter-bombed-out decor, began to fill the booth. Commerce commenced. Hours felt like seconds with the bustling of business and haggling of goods in full swing. By the time the crowds thinned and witches started migrating toward the ceremonial Mabon bonfire, the shelves were bare.

Vianna and Dee packed their booth decorations and loaded everything into the truck. The night wasn't over, though. Next was the bonfire, and the excitement that seeped from the witches gave the air an electric charge. Vianna grabbed a cloth sack filled with pinecones from behind the driver's seat, and Dee pulled out a velvet pouch from the glove compartment. Every witch was required to make an offering to the goddess at the bonfire.

"I'll show you mine if you show me yours." Dee waggled her eyebrows as they walked down the broken plank steps toward the rocky beach. "Well, smell mine might be more apt." She dangled the velvet bag in front of them, and a familiar scent filled the air.

Vianna barked out a laugh. "You're offering weed to the goddess?"

"Only the best for our lady."

The goddess wasn't so much a deity or person, but an essence that wove through the earth and all living things.

"Your turn." Dee nudged Vianna with an elbow.

"I tinkered with some pinecones so they'll give bursts of color when hit with fire."

Mother had always brought freshly killed carcasses, so a new tradition was needed. Pinecones weren't exactly awe-inspiring, but she'd run out of time and ideas.

"Color bomb-tastic!" Dee said.

Vianna snorted. "You'll be too high to notice."

Dee gave a good laugh but didn't argue.

Moonlight rippled across the ocean's surface, and the tide had pulled out to sea, leaving a coating of slick moss on exposed rocks. Witches mingled in clusters, some in pairs, a few on their own, and painted leaves or flames decorated their faces and arms. Some wore animal skulls as masks, and a few dressed in nothing but ornaments made of bones, shells, or tusks.

"The fire show last year was a joke. They better go all out this year if they want to keep their standing." Dee used the drawstring of the velvet bag to spin it around her finger as they walked.

The Fire Blessed Coven had prepared the bonfire show that kicked off each Mabon season for the past decade. They hadn't been around as long as the four founding covens, but they had enough clout to be acknowledged—as long as they put on a good show.

They approached a massive collection of branches that twisted into a towering tree, and at the base lay animal sacrifices, hex bags, bones, and crystals. The Tidal Coven huddled together on the west side of the fire. Frankie stood close to her coven mother, but her daughter wasn't present. On the east side stood the Mabon witches. On the south were the Lunar witches. They seemed more strategic with Ophelia standing in the middle and her witches forming a crescent moon around her. On the north side were the Original Blood witches, who seemed to be divided into several smaller groups, but they all had one thing in common: scowling at Vianna. Zosia stood behind her twin daughters in a neat little triangle. Tiphonie was off to the side on her own, her chin raised in self-importance. Behind the main covens were huddles of smaller, younger covens, watching.

A steady drumbeat began, deep and rhythmic. A witch with a

black-painted eye mask and a dress made of feathers all in fire hues stepped from the masses and blew a large horn that reverberated through the air. The crowd turned in unison, all eyes on the Fire Blessed coven mother as she approached. She wore a red, velvet dress, and a crown of burning candles sat atop her snarled, dark hair. Wax dripped down her hairline, but not a muscle flinched, her expression cut from stone.

Behind her came a line of witches who swung fire poi in swooping circles that dipped and weaved through each other, leaving lingering shapes in the air like a magical imprint. The crowds parted as they formed a circle around the constructed tree. After them came another group with large fire fans that they tossed into the air, then caught mid-flip.

The Fire Blessed coven mother stopped in front of the tree, and the drums stopped. She reached for a candle from her crown and placed it deep within the heart of twisted branches. As she stepped back, a single flame licked up the trunk, reaching higher and higher.

Whispered chants from the masses called for the energy of the goddess, willing her to accept their offerings. Solitary witches and entire covens alike chanted, but not in tempo or together. Instead, their chaos created a blanket of squirming whispers that pressed down on them. The single flame became a roaring bonfire that consumed the tree and stretched toward the stars.

The first wave of offerings was from the unbound witches, those who didn't have familiars. Coven-bound or solitary. For once, it didn't matter. Witches from all directions around the bonfire stepped forward and tossed in more bones, crystals, and small pouches.

Dee approached and tossed in her bag. She wasn't the only one offering weed to the goddess if the scent in the air was any indication. The smoke was also heavy with sage, St. Palo, and white willow.

A duo of witches in matching vests of animal fur and full-body ink tossed limp squirrel carcasses into the flames. Three Fire Blessed witches with painted masks broke from their circle. They carried cloth sacks like Vianna's, but instead of rigged pinecones, they pulled out bloody masses of tissue, each taking turns tossing chunks into the roaring fire. The last piece from their sack of blood was a fresh cow head that they all threw in together. It landed neck down with a wet *smack*, its unseeing eyes facing outward, reflecting the flames.

As more witches gave offerings, Mistress Layton broke from the Original Blood cluster and headed toward Vianna and Dee. "Ladies."

"Looks like the coven is extra divided tonight." Dee raised a brow at her mom as she pulled a thermos from her bag.

"Hmmm..." Mistress Layton nodded. "You know I can't speak of coven business, but things are often just as they seem, aren't they?"

"You always said if it walks like a duck, quacks like a duck, and stays in duck form in the presence of a coven, then it's a duck." Dee handed both Vianna and her mother collapsible cups from her bag.

Vianna grinned as she unfolded her cup. That was good advice. Dee poured steaming liquid for each of them, and when Vianna took a sip, Mabon cider coated her insides like an unfurling ribbon of fire.

They stood in silence for a bit, watching the offering pile at the base of the fire grow as the fumes thickened. Younger witches had begun to skip and twirl around the fire. Giggling, chatting, and energy swelled with every offering. The fire reached higher, and the dancing witches melted back into the crowds to make room for what came next.

"It's time. Hold this, dear." Mistress Layton handed her cup to her daughter, then patted her shoulder before stepping closer to the fire.

Older witches, the demon-bound, stepped away from their

groups to give their offerings. They stepped closer to the flame, palms raised toward the stars, and Vianna recognized every face. They looked different from when she was a child, more worn and smaller. Some weren't much older than her, but time had passed, and they'd earned mantles just as she had.

The crowd behind them grew louder. The Fire Blessed stomped their feet in rhythmic beats that shook the jangles around their ankles and slapped their thighs or chests. Other witches made varying animal-like sounds or humming noises.

Vianna's fingertips tingled with heat that felt hotter than the flames. Shuck was eager to come out. Her stomach flip-flopped with nerves. He wanted the door between them opened. Without a spell directing his magic, he wanted the chance to join in a crowd and choose his own actions. That was exactly what Vianna feared. Of all the places she could do that, this was the safest. He was among other familiars, other demons, and the witches who filled the beach knew the darkness of demons, welcomed it.

As familiars pressed closer to the surface, an inky blackness flooded the whites of their witch eyes. Eerie smiles of satisfaction spread over the witches' faces as they tossed items with etched symbols, and some sliced open their own flesh to offer blood.

"It is disrespectful to not let him out." Grandma Susannah appeared beside Vianna. "Disrespectful to *him*, not me. Nor them."

Vianna clenched her fists, which were stuffed into her pockets. She hated that Grandma knew what mattered to her, that it mattered *who* was being disrespected. Being demon-bound was the mark of a truly dark witch, who would undoubtedly do horrific things. And the ones who embraced their demon, who truly reveled in them—they became legends of darkness. Like Vianna's mother. But she didn't want to be a legend, not of darkness or any other kind.

Flames leape from the fire in fluid streams, landing in Mistress Layton's upturned palms. Her eyes were a shiny black as she stared forward. She hunched her shoulders inward, and the flame formed into the shape of a book.

A page made of fire unfurled from the book, materializing into a fire image of an older legacy witch who had passed. A Mabon witch stepped forward, crying, and blew a kiss at her lost mother. Then another page of fire flittered into the air, and a fire version of Josephine hovered above the book. Tiphonie let out a strangled cry, and Vianna turned to see that she was standing just a few feet away, her hand to her mouth and tears sliding down her cheeks.

A third page of fire flew up from the book, and Vianna's stomach tightened. She knew who she would see. A fire-formed Angeline was the last to materialize. Vianna clenched her jaw, no tear-streaked cheeks and no sobs of loss. Mother scowled down at her, knowing she didn't belong and, even worse, knowing she could belong. Vianna could become a legend, just like Angeline. That truth terrified her.

Her heart raced. She considered turning and walking away, never facing the demon now inside her or what he was capable of. But Shuck rumbled, and the marking on her collarbone burned so hot she flinched. They were bound. She couldn't run from him, just like she could never run from the ghosts.

She tried to shake the nervous energy out of her hands. She was going to let Shuck out, to understand what he wanted and what he would do. She had to if they were ever going to find a truce.

She picked up the cloth sack at her feet, wringing the top with both hands as she waited for her nerves to settle. Opening the sack, she tossed a pinecone into the fire, and an indigo flame burst toward the stars. No one turned in her direction or noticed. Vianna watched the displays as she continued to throw the pinecones, one by one.

A ribbon of fire looped from the bonfire and into Tiphonie's cupped palms before unfurling into a small fire-fox. The Parkers' familiar had passed through generations, just like Shuck and the

Roots line. It was rare for the same demon to stay with one line, and only a handful of witches in all of Salem could claim such.

Vianna shook her hands in an attempt to get rid of the jitters, then rubbed them against the stiff ridges of her black jeans. It was now or never. Her heart still pounded, but she exhaled and stepped forward, raising her palms in invitation.

Embers crackled like bouncing jellybeans, landing in her palms. She flinched in expectation of the burn, but there was no heat, only the warmth from Shuck swirling up her spine. The embers rose and looped in small circles, over and over, growing in tempo as they turned into flames. A shape began to form, and Vianna sucked in her breath against the tightening dread in her gut.

Flames looped into layers of silken fire petals the color of golden sunbeams and cherries as a stunning fire-peony bloomed. Vianna let out the breath she'd been holding, giving a small chuckle. She'd let the great, dark demon loose, and he'd made... flowers? Breathtaking flowers.

The peony rose from her palm as though caught in a breeze, floating up and spinning into long fingers of fire that reached upward, contrasting against the inky blackness of the sky. Vianna grinned, and Shuck sent a purr that rumbled through her bones. More flames jumped to her palm and as she imagined different flowers, Shuck molded each from flames. Roses, daffodils, daisies, and lilies of fire caught on an invisible breeze as they floated toward the moon. More and more flowers filled the air, until they were everywhere.

Every witch had stopped what they were doing to watch the flowers before tracking down to Vianna. She itched at the attention, as though pincher bugs swarmed beneath her skin. She looked up at the flowers still drifting in the air instead of at the narrowed eyes.

The flower petals began to contort, elongating and changing shape. When the new forms finished, she froze. The image closest to her was of a woman in a flapper dress behind a man on his knees. She gripped handles attached to a long wire wrapped around his neck. With a smirk, she yanked both handles in opposite directions. The man's hands flew backward, and she shoved a heeled foot between his shoulder blades, kicking him forward as she pulled backward.

Vianna's stomach churned. She knew the woman's face; her picture sat on the mantel at home. Grandma Maysel.

More flowers contorted, elongating, and Vianna couldn't look away. She was frozen, forced to watch as grandmas took shape through fire. Grandma Hannah wore a dress with layers and full skirts, but she could still swing an ax with ease. Grandma Annis had an elaborate collection of fans where she hid her blades. Her precision for finding organs on the first try was alarming. Grandma Victoria blew crushed powders on people. Grandma Francis had a body at her feet in the kitchen and cut pieces on a cutting board on the counter. Grandma Aileen sat by the bathtub, staring into the eyes of a body beneath the water.

Each warped flower made Vianna more sick in her gut. The air felt heavy, and her every breath was labored. She dropped her hands to her sides in defeat. The corners of her eyes burned and she blinked back tears. With a clenched jaw, she slammed the mental door shut on the connection to Shuck.

All of that murder. So many lives. And he'd showcased it proudly. He was a demon, so of course he was proud.

His growl shook every bone in her body. It didn't matter. He couldn't be trusted.

II

Save the Squid

Despite being exhausted from the witch market, Vianna only slept a few hours. She tried to focus on the prep left in the garden that still needed to be done before the first snow, but the memory of Shuck and his fire antics kept sneaking into her thoughts. After flopping this way and that, covering her face with a pillow to block the sunrise and shifting for a comfortable position a billion times, she whipped the blankets off and slid on a worn pair of black sweats.

Since she was up, she might as well be productive. She busied herself with unloading the truck and stacking their market acquisitions onto the shelves in the candle den. They'd made a good chunk of cash too, and she put half in the secret drawer in the conjure room and the rest under Dee's coffee mug.

No matter how much busywork she did, the multitude of faces flashing in her memory wouldn't stop. And not just her grandmothers, but the stares and whispers of every witch at the bonfire. Vianna and Dee had left right after Shuck's display, and the drive home had been quiet.

Vianna meandered into the backyard with a mug of steaming peach tea cupped in both hands. Mid-step off the deck, she paused, eyes narrowed at the flower bed that was supposed to contain fresh bulbs. "Damn it!"

Piles of dirt lined the edge, and bent pieces of chicken wire were tossed aside. Her grip on the mug tightened, and she had to stop herself from throwing it against the fence. She didn't want to just throw the mug; she wanted to kick something. Maybe the fence. She stomped over to the upturned soil and kicked at it with her bare foot, spraying clumps into the grass, and somehow that pissed her off too. And so she threw the mug at the porch in an explosion of porcelain shards.

"You worthless rat bastard pile of fluff," she growled at the trees. "I'm done playing nice. I'm going to make a hex bag that gives you poison ivy around your asshole and learn how to brew a potion that will make you a leper among your own kind!" She dropped her head with a huff.

Her eyes burned with the threat of tears, and she wanted to laugh at how absurd everything was. The squirrel was a little asshole, but he wasn't the one she was really mad at, and she knew it. Some part of her had thought she was different, that she could bond with Shuck and things would be different from the witches before her. But she wasn't different. She was just another tool for him to commit murder and mayhem. Why else would a demon be compelled to stay with the same line of witches for so many generations? Because they were the best tools for killing. And when had she become so naive with hopes and precious thoughts of being *different*? Now all she had was regrets: regret for caring, regret for hoping, and regret for trusting.

She tiptoed through the garden and picked out the pieces of her mug, flipping up the bottom of her shirt to hold them all. Back inside, she dumped out the mug into the trash and checked the time.

They weren't due at the tunnels until this evening, and she still wasn't sure what to make of their plus-one. Grayson saw too much, and it made her fidgety, like he could see the darkness within her.

Maybe she should call Tuck. She didn't want to trigger an invisible ward by bringing a cop. Vianna had just reached for her phone on the charger when Dee's screech sliced through the air. For half a second, Vianna froze, then she bolted for the stairs, taking them two at a time, and raced down the hallway. She yanked open the door, and a gust of old fish repulsed her back.

Dee was out of bed, a soft pink kimono hanging from her exposed shoulder, waving a teal wedge sandal at the ceiling.

"This means war!" She pointed the shoe at Vianna. "Don't you dare try to defend him. I knew he was stealing my stuff, but now he's ruined it! I'll never get the smell of fish guts out of the fabric!" She flung the shoe at the wall.

The drawers to her tall dresser opened and slammed shut in response. Dee glared at the dresser. "That did *not* sound like an apology."

Vianna sucked in her lips. She knew better than to talk when Dee was this riled up. A swamp-like mess of seaweed mixed with miniature-looking squid covered Dee's cherry blossom duvet. Tangled in the mix were teal shoes, scarves, and nail polish. Vianna picked up a bucket from the floor and turned it over to see the outline of a diamond stamped on the side.

"What is that?" Dee's voice was still in the shrill category. "The *Diamond*? As in the pirate ship?"

Oh. Understanding clicked into place for Vianna. "The spell. On the centerpiece at the market, the spell gave him access to anyone who stole." Which left a lot of questions. Why had he taken fingers immediately from Bun Head Witch but not Frankie? She was assuming it was Frankie, although it could have been another Tidal witch. The market had been full of so many people. But it seemed awfully coincidental. Frankie owned the *Diamond*, and that was the ship Shuck was now pilfering, if the bucket was a clear message.

Vianna looked at Dee. "I don't get it. She's a legacy and a pirate captain. Why would she steal candles or tea?"

"Maybe it's the thrill of stealing." Dee was still frowning at the mess on her bed. "It's a rush."

Vianna side-eyed her but decided to leave the questions of Dee's thievery experience for another time.

"What I want to know," Dee said. "Is why of all the things he could steal from that ship, he goes for this? What the hell?"

Vianna grinned. "It's like a dog bringing a dead bird as a gift. He's making nice with you." He liked Dee. Vianna felt certain of it. His pranks and teasing felt more like a sibling rivalry than an enemy attack. If he actually wanted to attack her, he could. Dancing fire images flashed back to life, and Vianna tried to shove them away.

Dee narrowed her eyes. "If you say so."

Vianna pulled up the edge of the sheets on the bed to haul the mess to the garbage. "I'll take care of this while you get in the shower."

"Wait!" Dee grabbed Vianna's wrist. "Those are glass squid. There's a ton of potions I can brew with those."

Vianna shook her head. "No way. I'm not leaving those in the house. They smell like rotten ass."

"Fine. Put them in the backyard, but sprinkle sea salt, alder twigs, and lemon zest over the top." Dee didn't wait for an answer, huffing off to the bathroom.

Turning her head away from the smell, Vianna gathered the mess within the sheet and hauled it out back. She emptied the spray-painted wheelbarrow of the quartz then plopped the stolen loot inside, along with Dee's instructions on how to preserve it. After three rounds of scrubbing, she finally just used what was left of the zested lemon to get the smell off.

Vianna's phone went off. "Who you gonna call? Ghostbusters!" She looked at the screen while drying her hands on the rainbow hand towel. Tuck was calling. Perfect.

She picked up the phone. "Hey. I was just going to call you."

"Good," Tuck said. "Because I need a check-in. I'm debating if I should come home now or in the morning. I'm tired and want to sleep, but I can make it home tonight if I need to."

"Oh. Well, I can't answer that. I can tell you that you have a ghost problem in the tunnels right below the shop, but I don't know its cause. Seems like it might be Ashley's doing, but it could be hoodoo or Google witches for all I know." She leaned a hip against the kitchen counter. "We're heading back tonight to do a little impromptu visit and see if we can catch anything she might be hiding. She wasn't exactly forthcoming or agreeable when I visited."

"Back up. What kind of ghost problem?"

"Well," Vianna said. "There's a whole gaggle of prostitutes hanging around. Feels like an old brothel."

Tuck snorted. "Not the kind of problem I was anticipating."

"Yeah. Me neither. And they're aware of each other and of me."

"And that's not normal?" Tuck asked.

"I think they died in a fire together, so maybe it makes sense for them to recognize each other. But not me. Only stronger ghosts can do that, usually the ghosts of witches." Thinking of the fire made her glance at the burn on her forearm. It was just a mark, already fading, and completely painless at this point.

"There's a difference?" Tuck asked. "Interesting. Out of curiosity, is the ghost of a practitioner different?"

Vianna browsed through the ghost library in her head. "I'm not sure."

"We'll put a pin in that for now, but I'm curious. In the meantime, it sounds like I should head home. Keep going with your plan to surprise Ashley, though. I'll be there soon."

"One more thing. We've also kinda picked up a plus-one. The ghosts have been harassing the shops next to yours, and someone called the cops. There's this detective, Elliott. I'm not sure I can shake him, and he plans on showing up tonight."

"Witches and cops working together? Geez, Vie. You trying to turn the whole world upside down?" Tuck chuckled. "All right. I'll be there soon, but call me if anything goes crazy."

"Will do. See you soon." Vianna hung up, tapping the phone against her chin as she thought. Ghosts of witches were different from regulars, but witches couldn't be the only factor. How did ghosts of hoodoo practitioners behave? Vianna had spent so long trying not to see the dead, it was likely she'd missed a few details.

There was still half a day left before they had to be at the tunnels, so she watched a YouTube video to help her fix the downstairs sink handles, reorganized the candle den, and took a shower. She was on her third cup of black tea when Dee announced she was ready to go. Vianna decided to act like the army getup—this time with an army jumper—was normal and perfect for the occasion. Mostly, she was just grateful that Dee didn't make her change out of her usual boots, jeans, and t-shirt. She also took a backpack with flashlights, batteries, matches, and a few spelled candles so she wouldn't have to ask Shuck for help.

Excited chatter about potions that contained glass jellyfish filled the Jeep as Dee drove them to the shop. Vianna nodded, trying to keep up, but mostly thinking of ghosts and actively not thinking of Shuck. They parked and headed toward Sticks and Bones.

Grayson was already there, leaning against the brick building and dressed very inappropriately. Granted, he was only wearing a t-shirt and jeans, but it was *how* he wore them. The shirt stretched over his chest and shoulders all snug, and his jeans were tattered and hugged him just right. Vianna's eyes tracked back up to his aviator glasses. Working together was a bad idea. He clearly didn't take his job seriously if he couldn't dress in a uniform that covered all of... *him.*

"We need to set more specific time frames." He pushed off the wall. "I don't like waiting."

"I haven't agreed to any type of regular meetups. Besides, sticking to a time frame isn't a thing with Dee around." Vianna didn't wait for a reply and pulled open the door to the shop, making the bell clank.

"I believe the phrase you were looking for is fashionably late." Dee followed her into the shop, Grayson behind both of them.

Vianna moved briskly through the rows of dream catchers, knotted scarves, and voodoo dolls, straight for the register in the back.

Ashley looked up, and her eyes widened as she slid off the stool. "What are you doing here?" She shook her head no. "No. Not now. You'll have to come back later. I'm busy."

"Shop looks pretty empty to me," Dee said.

Vianna shrugged. "Late, early, not invited, whatever. I'm here."

Ashley's eyes narrowed, but they'd focused behind Vianna. "Shit, Vie. I told you everything was fine, and you bring in PD, the narkiest narks ever." Ashley folded her arms and scowled at Grayson.

Dee snorted back a half-hidden laugh. Grayson only grinned, pulling off his glasses and looping them into his shirt. Whatever was going on in the tunnels was going on *now.* Vianna waved a hand at Ashley, uninterested in her chatter, and headed through the curtain to the back.

"Vie, stop!" Ashley bolted from her stool, but Vianna was already halfway down the hall. Dee and Grayson pushed past her too.

The hatch door in the pantry was open. Someone was down there, someone Ashley didn't want Vianna to know about. She was willing to bet the wad of cash from the market that it was Google witches. She had no idea how they'd called forth the brothel ghosts or what exactly they were doing with them, but she was about to find out.

Vianna lowered herself into the tunnels, one rung at a time, until her foot hit the ground. She looked around, noting that the candles were already lit. Dee climbed down next, with Grayson behind her.

Ashley hollered down from above. "I should lock you down there! Would serve you right. You know I can't leave the shop unattended."

The bell on the front door chimed, and Ashley turned and stomped off, muttering unintelligibly to herself. They all refocused on the cavern, and Vianna let her eyes adjust to the darkness.

"The air is bristling, like a firecracker just went off," Dee muttered into the thick, damp air.

"I feel it too." Vianna glanced at Grayson, who was rubbing his lower back. "You all right?"

He dropped his hand. "Fine. I don't feel... firecrackers."

"You wouldn't," Dee said.

"What does that mean?" Grayson unbuttoned the holster for his gun but pulled out a small flashlight instead, sweeping the cavern corners that the candlelight didn't illuminate.

"You can't feel magic," Dee said. "You're—ya know—a cop, and this is a witchy thing." She paused and looked at him. "Unless you *are* feeling something. Why were you holding your lower back like that?"

"Let's just focus on the case at hand." Grayson moved to the tunnel entries, shining his light down each.

"That's highly sus." Dee joined him and pointed to a tunnel. "That's where we found *clues* last time. Whatever is happening is probably happening in there."

Vianna smirked at the pause Dee took before saying *clues*. She'd wanted to say ghosts, but Grayson didn't know about Vianna's special sight. A door slammed shut, echoing from farther within the tunnel. Grayson motioned for them to step behind him. He placed one hand on his gun, still in the holster, and the other held up the flashlight as he walked crisscross near the wall. With a nod of his chin, he motioned them forward, and their trio moved deeper into the cavern.

Shifting through boxes, crates, and furniture wasn't the quietest activity, and Grayson did his fair share of glaring at their clamoring. When they emerged into the cavern, it was permeated with rose oil and whiskey. But this time, it was empty of ghosts. Vianna spun in a circle, confused. Come to think of it, the dueling Romeo and Romeo were gone too.

Bickering further down the tunnel drew her attention, and she pushed on further. Dee was right behind Vianna and almost made her trip. The three of them continued their trek until they ran into a closed door.

Grayson silently held up two fingers at them, then pointed to the wall. They looked at each other with a frown, then shrugged, unmoving. Grayson's lips thinned, and he held up his fist. Dee did a solidarity fist. He shook his head, stepped forward, and kicked open the door so hard it slammed against the wall.

Grayson tried to shove them out of the way, but Vianna shoved back, recognizing the person standing in the room. "James?"

12

It Ain't Funny

A blue-white light blinded Vianna for half a second before James pointed his camera at the dirt.

"Vianna," he squeaked, pushing up his night vision goggles. His two ghost-hunting buddies stood behind him. They wore matching crumpled, black cargo pants and t-shirts. Radio static sputtered in bursts from somewhere Vianna couldn't quite place, and small red lights flashed from a far corner.

Dee stepped into the cavern. "I guess we can scratch Google witches from the list."

"Google witches?" Liam echoed.

Grayson looked between them. "You know each other?"

"I didn't know you were going to be here." James rushed forward, his hands filled with a camera and large microphone. Cords spilled at his feet, right on top of a summoning circle spray-painted in construction orange in the dirt. "Not that it's bad. I'm glad you're here."

Vianna stopped with her toes just outside the circle. She stared down. "What *exactly* are you guys doing?" There was no way this group had summoned a full brothel of ghosts. Or had they?

"Our show." James gave an uneasy smile. "*Ghost Exposure*. Remember?"

"Not the brightest," Liam mumbled under his breath.

Dee walked around the circle from the outside, stopping at a mess of chicken wire strung between two metal poles, with solar panels at the base. "What is that?"

"Professional equipment. It's complicated." Liam raised his hand to stop the multitude of questions no one was asking. "Has to do with electromagnetic fields detecting ghosts. We've got this under control."

"So this is one of those ghost-hunting shows?" Grayson was playing catch-up. "Do you have a city permit to film down here?"

James and Liam slunk back, but Ruby spoke up. "Legally, we've done nothing wrong. We were given access to a private tunnel entrance by the property owner. I looked it up. It's legal."

That explained what Ashley was hiding, but why she'd risk Tuck's wrath by involving the shop was a mystery. There had to be something in it for her.

"That doesn't give you full access to the entire tunnel system to do whatever you want," Grayson said. "It doesn't work that way. Let's head back up and straighten this out."

"Vie." Dee pointed to the middle of the circle. "Isn't that one of yours?"

In the center of the spray-painted circle was a fat pillar candle with specks of color in the wax. Vianna tilted her head, narrowing her eyes to look more closely. She knew that candle, every part of it. The black was tourmaline, the drops of red were her blood, and the grit was granules of dirt from the jar of cemetery dirt she'd taken with her when she ran. The only unfamiliar part was the delicate chain wrapped around the outside of the glass jar.

The candle had been an experiment when she lived in Boston. Spelled candles had been around for centuries, and normally she wouldn't be able to instantly identify hers, but that candle had been unique. She'd been trying to make a spell to repel ghosts. It'd been her first attempt, and without a grimoire or proper help, the candle went awry. Instead of repelling ghosts, it attracted them. With limited direction in how to fix it, she'd abandoned the idea, tossing the candle in a forgotten drawer or closet.

"How did you get that?" Vianna couldn't even remember herself where she'd put it.

James handed the microphone to Ruby. "Taking something from the trash is not stealing."

"You went dumpster diving to steal Vie's candles?" Dee grimaced. "That's more than a little weird."

Vianna sucked her lower lip beneath her teeth to keep from yelling. "The only reason it was in the trash was because your uncle threw my stuff out before I could get it. So yeah, it's absolutely stealing."

Dee muttered under her breath, "Google witches would be better."

"Everyone out." Grayson motioned, herding everyone toward the way they'd come.

A match scraped against a box, and they all stopped, turning toward Liam. He knelt at the candle with a lit match.

"That's not a good idea," Vianna said.

"Start filming, James." Liam grinned and lit the candle. "We're not losing this opportunity." He stood, facing the camera James had raised in his direction.

Grayson leaned close to Vianna and whispered, "I don't know for sure the jurisdiction of these tunnels."

He'd been bluffing earlier about permits. Vianna would have smirked, but she was too concerned about whatever Liam thought he was doing compared to what he was actually doing. James looped his finger in the air to signal he was filming, and Liam's smile went from forced to beaming.

"We call to you, Elizabeth Derby West." Liam held his palms out as if communing with an ancient deity. Whoever Elizabeth was, he'd just trapped himself in a wonky spray-painted circle with her.

"That circle is whacked," Dee whispered to Vianna and Grayson. "It's a summoning circle, but—" She shook her head. "—it's missing the protection runes. It's not even quartered properly."

And it was huge, way bigger than needed and contorted to go around furniture that jutted into the circle. They hadn't even cleared the area.

"It's a circle of entrapment," Grayson said. "They're not supposed to be quartered."

Both Vianna and Dee whipped their heads in his direction. How did he know that? But before they could ask him anything, the temperature dropped, making Vianna's throat constrict from the cold. The smell of rose oil and smoke flooded the air. She swallowed the dry lump in her throat and rubbed her palms against her jeans. A careening howl sliced through the tunnels and every hair on Vianna's arms rose.

"Did you get that?" Liam turned to James with saucer eyes.

Everyone could hear it, not just Vianna. Her stomach tied in knots. That made for a seriously powerful ghost.

"Liam." Vianna's breath came out in a white puff. "You need to undo the circle. Counter clockwise motions in the dirt to disrupt the line."

Somehow, someway, the summoning had worked. But stepping over the circle or yanking Liam out would destroy any hope of containing the ghost. If anyone but Liam broke it, she'd be free to go at all of them. And after being burned by the brothel girl, Vianna really wanted to keep the mystery ghost on a leash.

Liam gave Vianna a wink before turning to the camera. "We're joined tonight by two Salem witches in the hope that they can help commune with Elizabeth Derby West. No one knows the hardships of Salem better than witches, so perhaps Elizabeth will feel a kinship with them."

James turned the camera on the three of them, Ruby swiveled blinding lights, and Vianna raised her hand as a shield.

"Camera down," Grayson barked.

"Liam!" Ruby shouted, aiming the light behind him. "The chair! It's floating."

The chair wasn't floating, but only Vianna could see the wispy figure with frizzy hair in a white nightgown. She let out another shriek, making veins of black spread from her eyes and mouth. In a blink, she threw the chair against the wall, and splinters of wood rained onto the dirt. The ghost vanished.

"Was that a hoax?" Dee leaned into Vianna. "Wires rigged or something?"

"No." Vianna shook her head slowly. "It's a ghost. And if that was Elizabeth, she's pissed."

"You want to let the pissed-off ghost loose?" Dee asked.

"No, but we can't leave him trapped in there with her. Remember the brothel ghosts?" Vianna lifted her burned arm as a reminder. "Whatever is going on down here, the ghosts can touch things. So the circle needs to be broken by the invoker to make her go away."

"So we're playing into this Elizabeth-the-ghost hoax?" Grayson asked.

Vianna decided now wasn't the time to address that detail. "Sure."

The marking on Vianna's collarbone warmed, and her fingertips tingled. *Shuck.* That was the last thing she needed to add to this mess. She pushed thoughts of him aside, and he sent a deep growl through her bones.

"It's okay to be angry, Elizabeth. We understand," Liam cooed as he walked the circle, not in the least bit afraid. Instead, his entire body bounced with energy.

Vianna looked around, trying to track the vanishing ghost. A cold whiskey-scented breeze swept through the cavern, carrying with it the brothel girls. Poetry Girl was in the lead as she swung a glass bottle, sloshing golden liquid at her feet.

"Chickaboo... I see you." The ghost twirled a finger at Vianna.

She kept her distance but watched Vianna with drunken, droopy lids from across the cavern. The other brothel ghosts kept their distance as well, making a clear division between the living and the dead. All except for one. Ruby fiddled with something behind a stack of crates, unaware of the danger that brushed up beside her. Elizabeth was contained, but the incoming fire was not.

Another high-pitched shriek made Vianna hunch her shoulders, and Dee squeezed her arm. Grayson flashed his light around the cavern, over the crowd of ghosts he couldn't see. The ghost of Elizabeth rematerialized, her pitch-black eyes tracking Liam. Smoke snaked into the cavern from the cracks in the walls, and Vianna's eyes burned.

"Dee, it's the brothel ghosts and the fire again. We need to get everyone out of here." Vianna coughed.

"Brothel ghosts?" James repeated. "Fire?"

Poetry Girl broke from the others, moving closer to Ruby as the smoke thickened. If the ghosts could pull Vianna into death loops, they could do it to others, too. There wasn't time to explain anything. Vianna bolted forward, swiping one of the loose bags of filming equipment on the ground and flinging it through the poetry ghost.

The bag flew through the wispy figure only Vianna could see and smacked Ruby in the face. With a gasp, she charged Vianna, landing a punch into her eye. Vianna crashed to the side and into wooden crates, spilling dried corn kernels everywhere as she fell.

Ruby shook out her hand. "What the fuck is your problem?"

"Ruby," Liam choked from inside the circle.

Dee ran over and kneeled in front of Vianna. She pinched her chin, angling her face this way and that. Grayson towered from behind, and Dee lowered her voice. "What was that? Why did you throw a bag at her face?"

A gurgling sound came from behind, and they turned toward Liam. A clawed hand with black-crusted fingernails gripped his throat, raising him into the air. He swiped out with his fists, and his feet kicked out against the ghostly figure of a woman in a flowing nightgown he couldn't see. She disappeared, and Liam dropped to his knees, gasping.

"Ruby, quick!" James yelled. "Turn on the REM pod."

James's handheld recorder blinked with a red light as he inched closer. On her hands and knees, Ruby slid a small canister toward the circle. The ghost flickered into view on the other side of the circle but stopped at the drawn line. She bellowed, then vanished. The air was so cold, it felt like breathing in ice shards, and the blinking lights on the canister went crazy.

The ghostly figure reappeared at the edge of the circle, black eyes staring at Vianna.

"Liam, you're not safe." Vianna didn't look away from the ghost.

"Elizabeth, we're not here to hurt you. We're not like the others." Liam's voice was raspy. He stayed on his knees, looking around. "We want to listen, not judge you."

The figure jerked her head to the side before vanishing, then reappearing directly in front of him. She leaned down, pressing her face closer to his, and let out an animalistic growl. Her frizzy, black hair blended with the thickening smoke around her.

"What was that?" Liam whipped his head from side to side, looking for what was right in front of him.

Brothel ghosts stumbled and giggled their way around the circle, some clinging to each other to stay upright. Elizabeth jerked away from Liam. Her nose lifted and her nostrils flared with a deep inhale. A thin spider-webbing of fog pulled from the brothel ghosts, making them wobble and groan—one falling to her knees. Vianna stepped away from the circle, closer to Dee and Grayson. What in Hades was going on?

Elizabeth took another deep inhale, this time her jaw dropping lower than any normal human. The white webbing from the brothel ghosts fed into her, and the wispy ghostlike edges of her formed into an almost-tangible person.

"Do you see that?" James yelled, keeping his handheld camera raised and steady.

Grayson pulled them further away from the circle, as though he could see the ghost. Vianna looked around, from ashen face to ashen face, and all of them looked terrified, like they'd just seen a ghost.

"Holy shit." Dee about crushed Vianna's arm with her grip.

Elizabeth's hand thrust out in a clawed attack, landing deep in Liam's chest. He bellowed, his body crumpling inward toward her hand and his foot kicking out behind him, disrupting the circle. Vianna ripped free of Dee's grip and rushed forward, but a wall of ghost fire roared up in front of her. The brothel ghosts screamed as fire consumed them.

"Dispel the circle!" she yelled to Dee. "He already broke it."

The air sucked everything in the cavern closer to the circle, furniture included, and dragged the brothel ghosts against the barrier of the circle. And just as fast, the air exploded back out, knocking everyone from their feet. Vianna's breath escaped her as she hit the dirt. Pain exploded across her body.

With a groan, she rolled to her hands and feet. Elizabeth still held Liam, but his body was slack. Ignoring the flames as ghosts melted, she crawled on all fours toward the circle. Using her hands, she swept at the spray-painted dirt in widdershins motions.

"You're ruining it," James screamed and lurched at her, but Grayson jumped in his way.

Vianna didn't hesitate, sweeping harder. Ruby stood as still as a block of cement, staring forward. Dee appeared on the other side of the circle, dropping to her knees and using her hands to swipe in the same motions as Vianna. James cursed at Grayson as they grappled behind her, but she focused on the circle.

Elizabeth howled, thrusting her hand deeper into Liam's chest, and he slumped into a heap on the ground. By the time Vianna and Dee finished cleaning up the circle, the ghost was gone. Liam didn't move. The smoke, fire, and brothel ghosts all vanished into nothing.

There was still screaming, and Vianna realized it wasn't any of the ghosts, but Ruby. Grayson rushed to Liam, his fingers sliding along his neck to check for a pulse.

"Dee, call 911." He lowered his ear to Liam's chest, and Dee pulled out her phone. "Vie, you have my back?"

Vianna froze. Have his back? Her? Against the ghosts or James? It didn't matter which. Either. Both. She nodded. "Yeah. I'm watching."

"Ruby, shut up!" James yelled, still recording. "I can't hear them."

Her screams deflated into whimpering as James hunched down, creeping closer to Liam's still body. Grayson placed both palms on Liam's chest and began CPR.

"Stay back." Vianna tried for her most stern tone, pointing a finger at James as though it were somehow threatening.

He hesitated, then pulled the camera back up. "Liam?"

Grayson continued chest compressions, then mouth-to-mouth. Vianna felt sick to her stomach. She couldn't think of anything to do but watch.

"Hello?" Dee held her phone to her ear. "Yes, we have someone hurt in the tunnels beneath Sticks and Bones."

"He's fine," James shrieked at Grayson. "Liam, come on. Get up. You're fine!"

Grayson pumped another round of chest compressions. "Badge number P7752. Tell them it's a P10-54."

Ruby's whimpering escalated to sobs as Dee repeated Grayson's words into the phone.

"Liam?" James yelled, dropping the camera to his side. "Liam! Bro, this ain't funny. Get up!"

13

Liquored, Fizzy, and Fruity

Grayson continued with chest compressions on Liam. Ruby cowered in the corner of the cavern, her sobs echoing down the candlelit tunnels. Everything else was still, so still.

Grayson pressed his ear to Liam's chest, paused, waited, then sat back on his heels and wiped his forehead with the back of his hand. "He has a heartbeat. He's breathing again."

"Holy goddess, that was intense," Dee said. "Did everyone see what I saw? Was that the ghost of Elizabeth?"

James let out a victorious yell as though he'd just scored the winning touchdown, and Vianna flinched. He didn't get it. This wasn't a game. Ruby crawled to the other side of Liam, her cheeks puffy and tear-streaked. She buried her face in his chest.

"This is gonna be gold, guys! I told you this case would make us famous." James paced the cavern, amped and jittery, his shoes crunching on the dust, shadows rippling and stretching along the rock-hewn walls. "I told you!"

Vianna's heart was still working on slowing to a normal pace.

Grayson stood, helping her up and nudging her and Dee away from Liam and his crying sister. Vianna scanned the ground again, but still didn't see the candle anywhere.

The police arrived quickly with paramedics, and she was convinced that the entire station had shown up, considering the number of bodies that were crammed into the tunnels. Grayson took the lead, organizing them into groups and coordinating to get Liam out safely. Dee had a cut on her forehead that was bandaged, and Vianna was given an ice pack for her eye.

Vianna and Dee migrated upstairs into the shop while Grayson was pulled into reports and discussions with fellow cops. Ashley sat at her usual perch, biting down her stubs of fingernails. Tuck stood beside her, his lips pursed so tightly he looked like he had none. He stormed over to them when they entered.

"Are you okay?" He was more barking an accusation than asking a question. "Your eye." His brow furrowed as he turned to Dee. "Your head."

"We're okay." Dee took a deep breath. "Have you heard if Liam is going to be okay?"

Tuck shoved his hands in his pockets with a frown. "No. What happened down there?"

It took less than a minute to catch him up. Surprisingly, Vianna did most of the talking. As the events in the tunnels settled into reality, Dee became more quiet. Her excitement over seeing a ghost had deflated when the cost was someone possibly losing their life.

"A ghost-hunting team." Tuck's voice had a rumble to it. "Let me guess, *Ghost Exposure*?"

"Don't tell me you watch it?" Dee asked.

"Of course not." Tuck's face pinched into a sour expression. "Ghost hunting disturbs the natural cycles around us. The dead are to be respected, not poked at like some freak show."

If that was how the hoodoo community felt as a whole, Ashely's actions were all the more confusing. "I'm guessing that means letting ghost hunters into the tunnels via your shop is not okay." Vianna focused on Ashley. "So what gives?"

Tuck raised his chin, looking around the shop until he found what, or who, he was looking for, then nodded to a far corner. "That's why."

Both Vianna and Dee turned to see Ruby talking with two uniformed officers.

"That's Ashley's off-and-on-again ex." Tuck shifted his jaw to the side in irritation. "I should have known when ghosts were involved. It didn't cross my mind until now."

Tuck's face went through a series of frustrated expressions. Vianna scanned the room for Grayson but didn't see him amid the sea of uniforms.

"Detective Elliott." A woman's sharp voice carried from the front of the shop as someone rounded the corner. She wore ankle boots, skinny jeans, and a buttoned-up blouse. Her black hair hung in silky waves at her shoulders.

Grayson ducked out of the hallway, heading straight toward her. "Captain Rodriguez."

They met in front of the hex bags, and the captain glared. "I suppose I don't need to say I told you so."

Grayson's expression was flat, giving Vianna no indication of what he was thinking. "This had nothing to do with them or the arrangement. A ghost-hunting team gained access to the tunnels."

Vianna straightened. The *them* in question was likely her and Dee. Maybe the captain didn't want witch consultants. It wasn't hugely surprising considering the centuries of antagonism between the two groups, but Vianna had assumed Grayson was acting off orders from higher up. Maybe he wasn't.

"And then what? Some innocent kid is attacked?" The captain turned from Grayson and headed straight for them.

Innocent seemed like a stretch for Liam or anyone in *Ghost Exposure*. But the captain hadn't seen the ghost, probably didn't even believe in ghosts. She likely thought witches were just some tourism ploy and didn't believe in demons either. As she approached, Ashley made her exit, sliding off her stool and slinking toward Ruby, who had stopped crying and was staring out the window.

"Which one of you is Ms. Roots?" Captain Rodriguez asked.

Vianna raised a hand. "Present."

"I don't like dead bodies or trouble, and you seem to attract both." There was no smile or hint of teasing.

That was a little unfair. But arguing with a captain in front of her uniform gang didn't seem like the best approach, so Vianna stayed quiet.

Captain Rodriguez straightened a row of candles shaped like skulls at the register. "Hmmm. No answer, I see. Odd, since Detective Elliott seems convinced you'll be a help to the department. I don't see it." She turned her back on them, facing Grayson instead. "Bring her to the precinct for a statement."

"She's my informant. I'll take her statement." Grayson motioned for Vianna and Dee to follow him toward the front of the shop. "Come on."

Vianna glanced at Tuck.

"I'll call you later." He nodded.

"Such a pleasure meeting you." Dee gave a mock smile to the captain as they walked away.

"I want that report by morning, Elliott," Captain Rodriguez called out to their backs.

Grayson held open the front door, and the three of them went outside.

"So when you hired us as consultants," Vianna said. "It was against the wishes of the SPD."

"It's complicated. I work with them for the moment, but not

for them. I don't play by the same rules." Grayson put his glasses back on. "I don't know exactly what happened down there, and I'm guessing you have more insight."

Dee snorted.

"Yeah," Vianna admitted. She wasn't ready to share all of her secrets with Grayson, but they needed to work together so more people wouldn't get hurt. What happened to Liam shouldn't have happened.

"I'm parked down the alley. Follow me? I know where we can talk."

"We're the orange Jeep parked in the lot off Cambridge." Dee pulled her keys from her purse.

Grayson nodded. "I'll meet you over there and you can follow me."

"Deal." Dee looped arms with Vianna and tugged her toward Cambridge Street.

They made it back to the Jeep, and Dee followed Grayson's shiny blue Chevy into a neighborhood with small brick-and-stone cottages nestled among overgrown foliage. He pulled into a driveway of a one-story gray house with a cherry-wood front door and matching window shutters.

"Is this his place?" Dee asked.

It certainly wasn't the police station. "Looks like it."

Last time a guy had taken Vianna to his place for dinner, things hadn't gone so well. She wiped her palms against her jeans and shook away the memories of Charles's calloused hands against her skin. Her stomach threatened to revolt. But she wasn't on her own, and Grayson wasn't Charles. Vianna looked at the window only to see Charles's face plastered on lawn signs for the election. She frowned. *Gross.*

Grayson walked over from his truck. His walk wasn't that of a puffed-up predator, but someone who owned whatever space he occupied and walked with purpose. Pulling off his glasses, he didn't shy away from eye contact as he approached. He wasn't staring them down, but he was seeing them, actually seeing and likely cataloging information into his mental files.

He tugged open Vianna's door, his gaze roving along her face and stopping on her eye. "Are you guys okay?"

She cocked a shoulder and slid out of the Jeep. "Fine."

"That's the universal I'm-not-fine-but-saying-I-am answer." Dee nudged her own door open. "Why do people do that?"

"I don't know," Grayson said. "Maybe habit?"

"Or maybe any answer doesn't matter because there's not anything to do about it. So, fine is just—" she shrugged, "—fine."

"That's depressing," Dee mumbled.

Overhead, long gray clouds framed the moon but didn't block out its luminescent glow. Salt permeated the air this close to the shore.

Grayson backed up to the edge of his lawn, hands in his pockets, watching them. "I wanted somewhere private to discuss what happened, and I thought by bringing you to my place, you'd get to know me a bit. Maybe we could even build some trust between us. Plus, I grill a mean steak, and it's a nice night."

Grayson's candid declaration left little to argue against. Although Vianna couldn't promise to trust him—she didn't even trust herself these days—she couldn't fault his reasoning. "I could eat. And some privacy is probably a good idea."

"You better have liquor, something fizzy, and something fruity," Dee said.

"You'll be lucky to find two of the three," Grayson said.

Vianna noticed the grin that edged the corner of his mouth and bit back her own as they walked up a stone path covered in overgrown weeds. He squeezed between them to the front door and unlocked it, then held the door open.

The living room smelled like those candles labeled fresh linen, just like he did, and moonlight poured in from the large bay window. A white suede couch filled the farthest corner, a weathered piece of wood hanging above it with a world map painted in faded hues.

The house had an open floor plan, and the kitchen and dining area were visible from the entrance. Dee headed straight for the fridge, and Vianna lingered at a corner bookshelf, looking at the framed pictures. There was an older couple she guessed were his parents. Several of a little girl. In one, she was blowing out a candle shaped like a six on a cake. In another picture, she was smiling beside a woman who was probably her mom. More pictures showed Grayson and a small group in army fatigues standing in a desert and the same group again at a marathon.

"Okay, time for some drink magic." Dee's voice carried from the kitchen as cupboards banged open and shut. "I need something to calm my nerves before we talk about what happened."

Grayson had followed her and opened a cabinet. "This is all I have for drinks."

"So you think." Dee shooed him out with a hand motion. "You're in the way."

There was a loud crash, and Grayson paused in his exit from the kitchen, taking a deep breath, then approached Vianna.

"She kinda takes over," Vianna said. "It's for the best."

He made a doubtful hum and stopped beside her at the bookshelf. The sliding door in the dining area slid open, and Dee meandered into the backyard, probably looking for more ingredients.

Vianna pointed at the little girl in the photo. "Daughter?"

"Niece." His eyes and smile lit up. "Aniyah is my sister's mini-me."

"They live in Salem?"

"They did." He nodded. "But Jayda died two years ago. Car accident."

"Oh. I'm sorry."

"Her husband, Malik, stayed in Salem, though, so I get to see them a lot. You have siblings?"

"Bless the goddess, no," Vianna said. "The Roots seed doesn't need to spread. We've done enough harm."

"I know a bit about the Roots women." His attention on her felt like an electric current, teasing her closer. "You don't fit the mold."

"You know an uncanny amount about legacy witches, especially for a cop."

"I do," Grayson said. "Let's get the steaks going and make sure Dee doesn't blow up my kitchen. Then we'll have a rousing round of twenty questions."

She followed him into the kitchen, where Dee was mixing drinks with a butter knife. "Mr. Two-out-of-Three is full of shit. There is no juice or carbonation anywhere in this place."

He raised a brow and pointed to the cutting board. "Looks like you found something fruity. Maybe you are lucky."

"I think the word you're looking for is resourceful. You've got a cranberry bush and a black oak tree. It's fall. My ingredients aren't limited to your health-freak ways. You are one, right? A health freak?" Dee handed a drink to Vianna. "Because there wasn't anything processed or sugary in any of these cupboards."

"Freak feels a bit dramatic."

"And you're a Hennessy man, I see." Dee held up a bottle. "The peppermint schnapps was a surprise. You like a little spice. That's good."

He moved into the kitchen and opened the fridge, packed with vegetables, and pulled steaks from a drawer.

"You've got enough produce in there to feed the whole neighborhood," Vianna said.

Grayson shrugged. "I like my veggies."

"I'll chop some up," Vianna said. "So we have more than steak and liquor." Not that a meal of steak and liquor was bad; she just needed something to keep her hands busy, instead of standing there fidgeting.

After prepping the food and drinks, Vianna and Dee settled into the picnic table out back. Grayson started the grill, then retrieved a fleece blanket for each of them. The view was phenomenal. The horizon was all ocean, and a small field of sand and beach grass separated his fenced yard from the shoreline. Outdoor globe lights lined the wrought-iron fence. Vianna burrowed into her blanket, appreciating the cool fall night. Dee's Hennessy-and-cranberry blend was the perfect combo of sweet and tart. Vianna poured herself a second from the pitcher Dee had brought outside for the girls since Grayson took his neat.

"Fill us in on how you know so much about legacy witches." Vianna shifted so that her elbows leaned against the table and she could watch Grayson's reactions as he organized his grilling tools. They were going to have to talk about the ghost, but she wanted a feel for his background and what he knew first.

"Same as you. Knowledge passed down from generation to generation." The steaks sizzled when he placed them on the grill.

"The surname Elliott doesn't appear in any coven records. You're not from a legacy line." Dee sipped her drink with narrowed eyes, tracking him like a hawk.

"Interesting." He turned to them, grilling tongs still in his hand. "You guys don't keep track of Hunters?"

"Hunters?" Vianna lurched upright. "As in, hunt down and kill demon-bound witches?"

All too casually, Grayson nodded. "Yup."

The Scandalous Divorce
of 1806

Vianna let the blanket slip down from her shoulders. Her leg muscles twitched, ready to flee, to bolt as fast as she could and get away from this demon Hunter. She needed a plan. Over the fence and across the shoreline was safest, but the tourist crowds weren't in this section to use as cover. And Grayson was in shape, a lot of in shape. She should never have trusted him, never come here. Because of that, she'd put not just herself but Dee and Shuck in danger too.

Dee nudged Vianna, slipping her satchel between them on the picnic bench and casually opening the flap as she kept her attention forward, watching Grayson as he flipped the steaks on the grill in a dark blue apron. There were some handy nuggets of defense in her satchel, but Vianna wasn't going there just yet. Grayson hadn't exactly charged at them, guns blazing.

"There hasn't been a Hunter incident in..." Dee's eyes glazed as she searched her memory. "Since the 1940s."

Grayson sipped his drink by the grill. "Depends what you classify as an incident. Keeping ourselves unnoticed by the general public has become one of our specialties."

Ourselves. There was an organized group, maybe even a full society of *Hunters.* What was next? Slendermen? Shuck was quiet. Either he didn't know about Hunters, didn't care, or was giving her the silent treatment. She focused her thoughts on Grayson. Had the whole consultant bit been a ruse?

She swallowed the lump in her throat. "Are you hunting me?"

"No." He shook his head. "Why would I grill steaks and announce what I was if I wanted to hurt you? And to be clear, we hunt demons, not witches."

But he knew she was demon-bound. "So why aren't you hunting me?"

Grayson chuckled, making the corners of his eyes crinkle. "Do you want me to?"

"No. I just—" Vianna bit back a groan. "What do you do if you're a Hunter who doesn't hunt?"

"I never said I didn't hunt. I said I wasn't hunting *you.*"

He pulled the steaks and veggies from the grill, then approached, keeping a wide berth, and sat on the opposite side of the table. "I haven't lied about any of my intentions."

Was he a mind reader now too?

"Working with you is a unique opportunity for the department. You're demon-bound. I can feel it. But that doesn't automatically put you on a hit list. Hunters have evolved with the rest of the world. We're more organized, and I get my orders from a branch in the government. There are no unsanctioned kills. We only go after those causing harm. The real bad guys."

"I'm not a good guy." Vianna didn't look away. She meant it. She'd never be now that she was bound to generations of murder.

Dee nudged her shoulder with an elbow. "Not helping."

"I hope you're wrong, because that would get awkward." Grayson scooped grilled zucchini and tomatoes onto his plate. "But I've got a sixth sense for that stuff, and you're not tripping any triggers."

"So the government controls Hunters. That seems like a bomb waiting to explode. You trust the suits?" Dee skeptically raised a brow.

He passed the plate of food to her. "It's complicated. But not all demons are the same, and not all of them are set on destroying humanity. Being a demon isn't enough in itself to be hunted anymore."

"Is the cop thing a ruse?" Vianna asked.

"No." Grayson took a drink. "I semi retired from a branch in the rangers that deals with paranormal issues. We handle infiltration and rescue. When I got home, there was a need in the department for my specialty, and my boss's boss asked me to step in."

"Semi retired?" Vianna asked and then immediately followed up with another question. "What need did the department have?"

"My unit earned some well-deserved, long-term time off. I could always get called back in, but the Salem PD's head of paranormal cases retired. So for now, I'm doing that."

She let his words roll around in her head. *All paranormal cases.* "That's why you showed up both times I called the cops. It wasn't a coincidence."

"No," Grayson said. "It wasn't. The Roots witches are well-known, and a call from that residence, or any other in that neighborhood, automatically means I lead the unit."

"What about when I hit your truck?" Her mind was tracing every time she'd encountered him, looking at all the details she'd overlooked. "What were you doing out there? You were right by the Legacy Cemetery."

"I didn't plan on you hitting my truck." His eyes locked onto hers. "But I was there because of your mother's funeral. I was gathering intel."

"What kind of intel?" Dee asked.

He cut up his steak into bite-size pieces. "A gathering of that magnitude drew in all the main players. I wanted to make sure they were who I thought they'd be, that I had the main family lines documented accurately."

"You were spying." Vianna didn't ask, but stated it.

"There's a lot of that going around," Dee said quietly.

He nodded, not denying any of it. No wonder he'd known she was a legacy. He understood more than she realized. A whole lot more. Dee finished her drink and leaned on the table with her elbows. Apparently, she didn't feel Grayson was a threat, despite his secret spying and hunting hobbies.

"Where does that leave us with the whole partner thing?" He nudged the serving dish toward Vianna.

She didn't even know where to begin. "Assuming you're not trying to kill me or the demon I'm bound to, I guess... Well, I don't know. It's been a big day. With whatever happened in the tunnels—which we still need to discuss—and now..." She set the plate down between her and Dee, rolling his words around in her head. "You've just told me you're the bogeyman that I didn't think existed."

Grayson folded a napkin into his lap, grinning the whole time and clearly amused. "Witches don't think Hunters are real?"

"Oh, we knew they were real," Dee said. "We just didn't think they were *still* around."

"So,"Grayson said. "Will you still work with me?" Suddenly, that all-seeing look he got made more sense. As a Hunter, he did see more than others.

She didn't have an answer to his question just yet. "Let's figure out the tunnels first, then we'll decide on the rest."

"That sounds practical," Grayson said. "In that case, I've got a few questions about the tunnels. Those idiots actually summoned a ghost? Elizabeth Derby West?"

"I meant to look her up." Dee pulled out her phone and typed on the screen. "That name was familiar."

"I've heard that name somewhere too," Vianna said.

"Oh." Dee's tone was not impressed. "That's why it's familiar. It was the article we read in the paper yesterday. The new exhibit at the Essex Museum."

Then Vianna remembered the article with the picture of Charles and Tiphonie. The new exhibit had been about Elizabeth. That couldn't be a coincidence.

"Let's find the goods on her." Dee's thumb swiped to continue scrolling. "Here we go. This looks juicy. 'The Scandalous Divorce of 1806.'"

"Is there a picture?" Hopefully of Elizabeth and not of Charles.

"Yeah," Dee said. "And I think it mostly looks like her. A little less creepy than the ghost version, but similar." Dee flipped her phone over, showing both Vianna and Grayson the portrait.

"Looks like her to me," Vianna said.

Grayson shook his head. "Ghosts aren't in my norm. Do they all look that bad?"

"I don't think death is ever a pleasing sight, but she's more creepy than most." Vianna pulled the blanket back up around her shoulders.

Dee's eyes flicked up from her phone to Vianna, then back down. "Listen to this. Elizabeth was one of the first women in Salem to be granted a divorce from her husband while retaining her inheritance. But to get the ruling, she needed proof of infidelity, so she marched *a parade of prostitutes from the local brothel* into the courtroom."

That answered a few questions. "So the brothel ghosts must be attached to Elizabeth." Which wasn't the biggest surprise after seeing her feed off them, if that was what she was doing.

"Brothel ghosts?" Grayson asked. "There was more than one ghost down there? And you could see them?"

Oh. That. Needing a second longer to gather her courage, she let the silence linger for a good minute or two. If Grayson was a Hunter, that meant he believed in demons and knew that magic was real. Maybe ghosts wouldn't be that weird for him.

"Yeah." Her voice was a rough whisper. She cleared her throat and spoke at a more normal volume as she reached for the tongs to spoon food on her plate. "There were more ghosts, and I could see them."

"That doesn't sound easy." His voice was soft. "Did you inherit that from your dad's side?"

"No," she blurted, then cringed. Her knee-jerk reactions weren't always honest. "I mean, I don't know."

Dee suddenly became riveted by the food on her plate, avoiding eye contact with either of them.

"You never looked into the other half of your DNA?" Grayson took a bite of food.

She picked at a zucchini on her plate with a fork. "Sometimes finding answers doesn't make things better." Her father was dead, likely killed by her mother, and learning the details wouldn't change anything.

They ate in silence, listening to the sea grass rustle and the waves lap at the shore as everyone digested different bits of new information.

Dee used the pitcher to refill everyone's drink. "So the case is still ongoing, right? We're gonna figure out how to stop this, right? So no one else gets hurt."

Grayson finished a bite of food as he nodded in agreement. "I'm in. But I've never hunted a ghost. Any tips?"

She put her napkin on her plate and pushed it away. "I'm not sure ghosts can be hunted."

Grayson leaned his elbow on the table. "Is she a typical ghost?"

"No." Vianna thought about how Elizabeth seemed to feed off the other ghosts. "Not at all. She's stronger, and others could see her besides me." That had happened right after she'd drained the brothel girls. It had to be why she'd gained enough corporeal strength to be seen.

"That never happens?" Grayson asked.

"I wouldn't say never. Ghosts of a witch tend to be more aware and occasionally able to move things. But not shatter chairs against walls." Vianna sipped her drink.

"But," Dee said. "Her name isn't in any of the coven logs, and they predate her time. I don't think she's a witch."

"What about other types of ghosts?" Grayson picked up his plate and cup, heading toward the house.

"I've been wondering that lately too." Vianna scooped up the pitcher with her dishes.

Dee grabbed a serving dish and stacked it beneath her plate. "You were?"

"Yeah," Vianna said. "Tuck asked about ghosts of practitioners, but I don't think that's it either."

"What about the ghost of a demon?" Grayson used his elbow to push the sliding door open.

Vianna followed him in, trying to picture how a demon-ghost would appear. "Demons don't have ghosts. At least, I've never seen one. What does a demon even look like without a host?"

"Usually darkness. Sometimes they can take a shape, sometimes not." Grayson stacked dishes in the sink. "What about the ghost of someone who was taken by forced possession? A witch willingly bonds, but isn't possessed. They're more like a conduit, but you said that still affects their ghost. The ghost of someone who was full-on possessed—that has to affect a ghost even more."

"You sound pretty confident in that." Dee handed over her pile of plates, then took Vianna's and handed those over too. "You noticed something, didn't you?"

Vianna slid onto the wooden stool at the other side of the counter, watching Grayson as he rinsed the dishes.

He dried his hands on a checkered dish towel. "When she materialized enough for me to see, I noticed the black bleeding from her ears and deep bags under pitch-black eyes. She looked like a lot of possessions I've seen."

Vianna twirled her thumb ring, her mind spinning.

"What are you thinking, Vie?" Dee asked.

"I don't know. Is that why the ghost can move to areas beyond its death cycle? Why here? Why did James and his entourage pick this ghost? I've got nothing but more questions."

"I'll do a background check on the ghost team, and I'll check the Hunter logs for anything that fits around the time of Elizabeth Derby's death."

"Hunter logs?" Dee perked up.

"Don't even ask." Grayson raised his palms in defeat. "I can't get you access to those. But I'll let you know if I find anything."

Dee pouted. "I'll check newspapers or any historical documents that have anything about illnesses or doctors for Elizabeth. There probably won't be much from that long ago, but I'll see if there are any photos of her wearing that necklace wrapped around the candle."

"I'll check in with Tuck. See if there are any more details I can get on how to send Elizabeth back where she came from." Vianna slid from the stool, and Dee straightened.

"You ready to go?" Vianna asked her.

"Yup," Dee chirped. "I love me some research."

Grayson walked them to the door. "Let me know if you hear anything else."

"Will do," Dee said.

"And Vianna," Grayson said, and she turned back. "Put some ice on that eye. It's swelling."

She frowned and waved him off. "Talk soon."

They got in the Jeep and left Grayson's. Dee was quiet most of the drive home. "I didn't see that one coming. Not for miles."

Vianna assumed Dee meant that Grayson was a Hunter. "Me either."

"Hunters, killer ghosts, people getting hurt..." Dee trailed off. "It's been a day."

"Mm-hmm." Vianna rested her head against the headrest.

Dee turned off Main Street, onto Heritage Way. "It wasn't what I thought it would be."

Vianna stifled a yawn. "Grayson's place?"

"No." Dee frowned as she pulled the Jeep into the driveway. "The ghost."

Vianna didn't reply, unsure of what to say. She stretched out her neck and shifted in the seat. It'd been a long couple of days.

"Seeing a dead body isn't too out of the norm for someone raised as a legacy witch. And I kinda assumed it would be like that. Or watching a dramatic movie." Dee turned off the Jeep and turned to Vianna. "It wasn't."

After a long pause, Vianna said the only thing that made sense to her. "I know." She knew all too well.

15

A Police Escort

Vianna managed a few hours of sleep, enough to keep her coherent the next morning. Another hour or two and she'd be ready to tackle the world. She was nestled on the couch with a blanket, her toes snuggled between the cushions, as Dee finished her last cup of coffee in the kitchen before heading out to work.

"Elizabeth decided to crash my dreams last night. I'm not a fan of her look. Are they all that creepy? With the black eyes? She charged me with supersonic speed." Dee made a pinched face. "I kinda get your sleeping issues now."

"She's an especially creepy one," Vianna said.

"I've got to be at the cemetery in a half hour. The dead zone for cell service out there means I won't be able to look more into this demon theory until later tonight."

Vianna wiggled deeper into the couch. "Okay. Try to cut out early if you can. There's supposed to be a storm moving in." Maybe she could just hide under the blanket all day, take a personal day and hide from all the crazy. She'd heard of people taking personal days. It was a thing.

"Wait until I get back to cause more trouble." Dee patted Vianna's shoulder as she headed toward the door.

"I'm taking a time-out from trouble." Vianna nodded as if saying it out loud made it official and real.

"Uh-huh," Dee said. "Sure. See you later." She left.

Her muscles relaxed, and she was beginning to think this whole take-a-day-off thing was possible.

"Nothing but an ungrateful loiter-sack." Grandma's voice came from beside the couch.

Vianna squeezed her eyes shut.

"Don't pretend like you can't hear me," Grandma hissed. "I'll use a tooth stick to clean out your ears."

With a groan, Vianna flung the blanket off her. "I wish I couldn't hear you."

"Only dolly-mops sleep the day away." Grandma hovered close by.

Vianna stood and headed into the kitchen for her phone. She wanted to check in with Tuck. Maybe he'd heard more about Liam, and she was also hoping he might have ideas about how to deal with a summoned ghost.

He answered on the second ring. "Hey. You guys make it home all right?"

"Yeah," Vianna said. "Cops leave your place in one piece?"

"Just barely. Sorry to drag you into all of this. I'd thought I was sending you in on story mode," Tuck said. "I didn't realize we'd already leveled up to a raid boss."

Vianna chuckled. Maybe seeing the past and the future tangled together was a story mode of sorts. She paced back to the living room, picking up her empty mug and taking it to the sink. "Have you heard anything about Liam?"

"Ashley called the hospital, lied and said she was family to get information," Tuck said. "The doctors aren't sure if he'll wake up. He's out of surgery, though, and it was a success. I was planning on stopping by in a bit to see if I can't help him wake up."

Help him wake up was an interesting phrase. Tuck was talking about hoodoo. Vianna normally tried to stay in her own lane, not pushing herself into others' business, but there was a lot she didn't know about ghosts, and not knowing was making things more dangerous. Dee had been right. She sucked in her insecurities with a deep breath.

"Can I come?" she asked.

An awkward silence followed her question. She assumed he was thinking, so she gave it a minute. She picked at a bundle of lavender hanging by the kitchen window above the sink.

"Okay," Tuck said. "I've got to finish up some things here, so meet me there in two hours?"

"Deal. Oh, and if you see a black candle with a chain wrapped around it, put it aside for me. I think it's what James used to summon the ghost."

"Like a trigger object?" Tuck asked.

"A what?"

"It's a sentimental object from their life that a spirit will attach to," he said.

She hadn't heard it called that, but it made sense. The cinnabar ring she used as a talisman had been easy to attach to Grandma. Maybe this wasn't just about the spell in the candle, but the chain wrapped around it. Or both.

"Can we un-attach a ghost from a trigger object?"

"Theoretically," Tuck said. "If we can destroy it. I'll need you to pick up some ingredients."

"Not a problem." Vianna opened the junk drawer and shifted around for a pen and scrap of paper. "Give it to me."

"Chaparral oil, pokeweed root, and myrrh gum. Is the candle tied to you in any way?"

"Yeah," Vianna said. "It's an oopsie mistake. Has my blood in it."

"That a big oopsie. We'll need graveyard dirt from one of your ancestors."

Vianna jotted everything down. She was out of graveyard dirt and would have to swing by the cemetery. It would have been a lot easier to text Dee if cell service worked. "I'll pick up the stuff, then swing by the hospital."

Knocking shook the front door, and Vianna jumped. She was used to Shuck warning her about that kind of stuff, but he was silent.

She crossed to the living room. "I gotta go. I'll see you in a bit."

"See you soon."

Vianna hung up the phone and peeked through the curtains of the bay windows at the front of the house. She frowned. Two officers in dark blue uniforms stood at her front door, neither of whom were Grayson.

"Do not open the door for them." A chill washed over Vianna as Grandma Susannah appeared by the window. "Go call Zosia. Have her send the coven. Don't let them take you like they did me. Don't let them win." Grandma's voice cracked, and for a moment, she seemed afraid. But in a single heartbeat, the vulnerability disappeared, and she set her face into its normal grimace and clenched her jaw.

"Watch the side gate?" Vianna was hoping to distract Grandma before opening the door, because she couldn't just ignore the cops. Luckily, it worked, and Grandma vanished.

Vianna opened the front door with a loud creak, and a gust of wind whipped through the house. "Can I help you?"

"Vianna Roots?" the shorter officer asked. He had a thick, untrimmed mustache that matched his eyebrows. His partner had skin as pale as a ghost and matching white hair that caught in the wind from the brewing storm.

She was tempted to say they had the wrong house, but she was working with Grayson now and wasn't ready to burn bridges with all his demon connections. "That's me."

"Is Sandeen Layton here?" the mustache cop asked.

"No." Vianna folded her arms over her chest. "She stepped out."

"We're supposed to pick you up for questioning. Captain's orders."

Vianna arched her neck to see behind them. A shiny squad car sat parked in front of her house with the large SPD on the side. She could practically feel her neighbor's beady eyes peeking from behind their curtains. She looked back at the officers with a raised brow. They'd just announced she was working with the cops on a bullhorn. She couldn't help but wonder if the captain had thought this all the way through.

"All right. We'll try it this way." She was under the impression she'd already done questioning with Grayson at his place, but maybe she was missing something in this new process. After pulling on her boots and jacket, she followed the officers down the walkway.

"Everything all right, Vianna?" Ophelia stepped onto her porch.

Now Vianna was positive the captain hadn't thought this through. Vianna might be an outcast to her own kind, but witches handled their own problems, even outcast problems.

"I'm fine." The grip on her arm from the cop escorting her wasn't all that encouraging.

Ophelia raised her voice over the howling wind. "I expect to see you home soon."

The taller white-haired cop stood guard, hand on his holstered gun, as the mustache cop put a hand on her head and pushed her into the car. Her door was slammed shut, and they quickly got inside and drove away, clearly anxious to get moving.

They didn't say a word on the drive, and a dread grew inside Vianna's gut. The back of the squad car was made of a weird plastic with a metal cage between her and the cops, as though she might surge and attack them at any moment.

They pulled into the station, and once they had her out of the car, they kept a grip on her arm as they walked her into the building. The reception area was thick with the smell of burnt coffee. A woman with rosy cheeks and purple nails tapped away on a keyboard behind a tall counter, and the wall behind her had framed portrait photos of officers in uniform. Above the frames hung a large plaque reading 'In Memory Of'.

Three ghosts had been shot and killed in the lobby; two seemed like citizens in casual clothing, and one was an officer in uniform. Vianna focused on the receptionist instead of the phantom splatter of blood and chunks of flesh across the wall to her right, on repeat.

When the woman looked up from her monitor, she didn't give Vianna the time of day, but grinned at the taller officer. "Welcome back, Charlie. All cleared."

The metal door to the left unclicked—the receptionist must have pushed a button to give the okay. After they walked through, the door clicked with a lock behind them. The hallway opened up to a large room with officers who shuffled papers and clicked at their keyboards. The far wall was filled with more portrait photos of officers in uniform, and the plaque above these read 'Salem Police Department'. Vianna did a quick scan for Grayson's face and found him toward the top.

A few groups of uniformed officers clustered together outside the offices. As they walked through rows of metal desks, the hairs on Vianna's arms rose. Every set of eyes tracked her, unashamed to be staring at the witch. She wouldn't be all that surprised if there was a stake in the back to burn her.

Her escorts took her by a wall with a giant cork-board filled with patches that had the names of cities from all over and then around a corner to another hallway. The mustache cop opened a nondescript door and nodded his chin inside. She entered a gray room with matching gray tiles. A desk and a few chairs sat in the middle, but nothing else. The door slammed shut behind her, and a lock clicked.

Did they really just lock her in? Vianna stood for a moment, staring at the door and assessing what level of danger she was in. Her fingers twitched, wanting to feel the pinpricks of energy from Shuck to know she wasn't alone, and she almost pulled on their connection but resisted. She was fine. Mobs didn't hang witches anymore, and apparently even Hunters were less inclined to kill them for no reason. For now, she was just fine.

The room had a sterile bleach smell. There were no windows, and a camera blinked red in the corner. Her heart rate thudded. After a good fifteen rounds of pacing as she counted her breaths, the adrenaline finally eased, leaving room for her to remember that it'd been a day and a half since any sleep. She slid into the chair and let out a long breath, rubbing her eyes.

With her panic calmed, she realized something else about the room. There were no ghosts. There were no dismembered bodies or victims tortured by her ancestors. There was nothing. Suddenly, the room didn't feel so scary, but oddly comforting.

She rested her arms on the table and lay her head down for just a quick moment. Her body slumped with an exhale. There were no ghosts splattering blood or chattering about every one of her faults. Her lids grew heavy, and she stopped resisting sleep.

16

Ghost Repellent

The door slammed, and Vianna bolted upright in her chair. Captain Rodriguez stood by the table, holding a folder stuffed with a thick load of papers. "Didn't mean to interrupt your *nap*."

Perhaps her snippy tone was normal for her, or perhaps she really, *really* didn't like witches. Either way, it didn't really matter. Vianna rubbed the sleep from her eyes. How long had she been out? She pulled her phone from her pocket. According to the clock, she'd been out for almost an hour.

Rodriguez cleared her throat, and Vianna looked up. What had she said? Apologizing for waking her? "It's okay. I have weird sleep patterns." She tucked her phone away. "Don't worry about it."

The captain's lips thinned, and she set down a recorder, piece of paper, and pen. "We'll go over your statement, and then I need you to write it down."

"There's not a whole lot to say." If this woman thought Vianna was going to go on record about seeing ghosts or being a witch, she was confused. Did she even know Vianna could see ghosts? Did she think witches were just a tourist gimmick, or did she know they were actual demon-connected magical killers?

Vianna decided to give her the safest version of events. "We ran into some TV ghost team in the tunnels, and they were pretty chaotic. Their gadgets flashed and beeped like a carnival." Vianna flashed her fingers to mimic it. "They were shouting and kinda freaking out. It was all very confusing. Then the one grabbed his chest and crumpled to his knees." It was all true.

"Why were you in the tunnels?" Rodriguez sat in the chair opposite Vianna.

That was an odd question. Didn't she already know? "Because there'd been noise complaints."

"So you decided to reach out to Detective Elliott for help? Had you two worked together before, and that's why you were comfortable contacting him?" The captain tried to act bored by the question, but her eye contact was off, like she was looking just to the side of Vianna instead of actually at her.

"This was my first time working with Officer Elliott." Vianna could tell when she was being probed for information, and she wasn't about to offer anything for free. Knowledge was more valuable than gold.

The captain thumbed through her folder of papers. "Officer Elliott is accustomed to running his own team, and he's adjusting to our department's way of doing things. I'm not convinced that working with you is the best move to better serve our community. Your lack of... legitimacy brings our competency into question."

So she was on the witches-are-a-tourist-gimmick side of things. Which also meant she might not even know Grayson was a Hunter. Vianna had stepped into a steaming heap of something without even realizing it.

"You should tell him the arrangement isn't going to work for you. It's not really your kinda gig, anyway, because I'm sure you don't want the police in your business, watching your every move, what with how often dead bodies show up around you." The captain didn't even bother to fake a smile.

That was pretty mild as far as threats went. Vianna wasn't agreeing to anything. She didn't trust the captain. "I'll keep that in mind. Anything else?"

"Don't forget to consider your neighbors, Ms. Roots. They're of the same stock as you, isn't that right? You all scam tourists to make a quick buck. I'm sure they wouldn't appreciate the extra attention."

Vianna stared at the woman, not offering a single word or the slightest muscle movement. Either the captain had the biggest set of balls Vianna had ever seen, or she was the most clueless human ever.

"For everyone's best interest," the captain said. "Get out of your agreement with Detective Elliott."

The door to the interrogation room slammed against the wall, and Grayson stood in the doorway. He looked ready to pound something with his fist. "Rodriguez, this is not how things are done." He took a deep breath, nostrils flared, and turned to Vianna. "This won't happen again. Come on, I'll give you a ride home."

He wasn't getting any argument from Vianna. She hopped up. "I'll meet you outside." Whatever fight they were about to have, she didn't want to be a part of it. The sooner she got out of there, the better.

"No need. I'm leaving with you." Without a word to the captain, Grayson turned and followed Vianna out. He jerked a key card against a sensor to open the doors and gestured for her to go first.

When they made it outside, the overcast clouds had deepened from a light gray to something angrier. A light rain misted her, and she held up her hands to shield herself.

Grayson pointed to his truck in the parking lot. "This way."

She jogged after him, and they both quickly got in.

"You should have called me." He used the bottom of his shirt to wipe the rain from his face.

"How was I supposed to know that?" She shook out her hair. "You're a cop. They're cops. This is the cop station."

"Well, now you know. You're never debriefed by anyone but me. You'll never be asked to write anything down or make any official statement." He started the truck and turned on the heater. "And she's damn lucky it didn't start a war with your neighborhood."

"The verdict is still out on that one." Ophelia had looked all shades of displeased.

They sat there for a moment, both quiet. Vianna checked the time on her phone again. She was supposed to meet Tuck at the hospital in twenty minutes. She'd have to hit the cemetery after the hospital instead of before.

Grayson took a deep breath. "No one in the department speaks for me or acts for me."

Vianna chewed on her lip. "Okay." That was probably for the best since the captain seemed ready to start a war she didn't understand.

Grayson didn't move, just sat there with his eyes forward on the station.

She didn't mind sitting in silence or giving someone room to think, but she kinda had somewhere to be. "I was supposed to meet Tuck at the hospital. So I have to get going."

He leaned against the steering wheel and turned in her direction. "I'll drive. I checked the Hunter logs and didn't find anything on Elizabeth, but there were a string of deaths after hers that were marked as demon activity. I called the hospital to have Liam's doctor run some specific tests, and I need to swing by to pick them up."

"Oh." That was a lot of information. Hunters could verify demon activity by medical reports. And wherever the Hunter logs were, they were close by. "Let's go."

Grayson turned on the windshield wipers, and they headed out of the parking lot. Vianna texted Tuck to tell him she had Grayson with her so he'd have a heads-up. She wasn't sure where practitioners stood with cops, but Ashley hadn't seemed thrilled by them.

When they pulled into the parking lot of the hospital, Vianna took a deep breath to help prepare herself. Her plan for survival was to find any ghost-free areas and focus there. They got out of the truck and jogged toward the main building. Vianna didn't even make it to the door before strolling by a mangled human form: a teenager crumpled on the pavement by the entrance where he'd bled out. Vianna sped up, keeping her line of sight up and away from the body, until she careened into Grayson.

He didn't budge, steadying her with a hand around her waist. They were both getting wetter by the minute, and his shirt clung to every stupid muscle.

"You all right?"

Vianna straightened, then nodded. "Yeah. Just got distracted."

With a frown, his hand slid from her side, and the automatic double glass doors behind them opened. She broke apart and jogged into the building with him right behind her. Her clothes were almost wet enough to wring out, and she wiped the excess water from her face and neck.

"They've got towels at the nurse's desk," Grayson said. "I'll get Liam's room number too."

Vianna nodded. Antiseptic fumes clung to her pores like plastic wrap. She looked around the waiting room, filled with several rows of seats wrapped in plum fabric pressed against each other and vending machines for soda and candy that lined the back wall. The living fidgeted with their clothes or hair, nibbled their fingernails, or bounced a knee, but the dead were completely motionless. Some of the ghosts stood, some sat, but every one of them faced the same window that overlooked the parking lot, their eyes wide and unblinking.

Vianna's footfalls turned toward the waiting area, pulled toward the ghosts and the window. Breathe in, step-step, breathe out, step-step. Breathe in, step-step, breathe out, step-step. Bright lights came from the window, and Vianna turned with a hand up just as a car crashed through the wall, raining chunks of plaster and shattered glass over every person. Vianna dropped to her knees, covering her ears from the screams competing with the constant long honk of the car tilted on its side. A heavy copper smell bled through the air, and a bone-shuddering *creak* of warped metal made her cringe.

"Vianna!" Grayson's hands wrapped around both of her arms, pulling her up from the ground. Concerned warm brown eyes looked down at her.

Her breathing calmed, and amazingly, all of the ghosts washed away. The broken, bloody bodies crushed by the car crash only Vianna had seen faded away as though an invisible tide took them out to sea. Even the car dissipated. But the living remained and gave her a wide berth, avoiding eye contact.

A rail-thin Hispanic male in maroon scrubs with full-sleeve tattoos stepped up beside Grayson. The nurse pursed his lips at Vianna, then handed two towels to Grayson. "You guys okay?"

"Yeah." Vianna took a deep breath and accepted the towel Grayson offered her.

The nurse shrugged and left. Grayson's lips were tightly pressed together, and he didn't say anything. She was grateful, considering all the people actively pretending like they weren't side-eyeing her.

"You okay to go check on Liam?" Grayson asked.

Vianna nodded. "Yeah. I can do this."

"Come on. He's in room 408." He gestured to the doors at the left of the check-in desk.

The ghost of an elderly woman with large fluffy slippers meandered closer, but anytime she got within a few feet of Grayson, she'd look around with a pinched, dazed expression and back away.

"Vie?"

She turned away from the ghost. "I'm good. Let's go."

They went through the double push doors that read General Patient Rooms. The long hallway on the other side had laminated floors, and the walls were painted in sage with framed photos of trees. Two doctors in white coats passed them, chatting about a scheduling problem with Operating Room 3.

Halfway down the hall, a ghost collapsed to his knees just outside a doorway. Vianna veered to the side to avoid walking through him, but the death loop was interrupted as Grayson passed by, and the ghost faded into the room. They stopped at the elevator at the end of the hall.

"Do you want to talk about it?" Grayson pressed the button with the up arrow, and it lit with yellow light.

That meant she was doing her weirdo look that made people think she was crazy. She straightened and tried to clear her expression to something neutral. "Talk about what?"

He adjusted his watch, then stuck his hand in his pocket. "Whatever has you strung out."

Strung out? Great. He already knew she saw ghosts. Pointing out the obvious wasn't giving him super secret intel.

"A lot of people die at hospitals, which creates a lot of ghosts." Avoiding eye contact, Vianna stared forward at the advertisement for Tempur-Pedic pillows plastered on the outside of the elevator doors.

"So seeing ghosts is an all-the-time thing?" Grayson stood by her, also staring forward. "Everywhere you go?"

"Yup. Won the lottery on that one."

The elevator doors opened to a ghost flat on her back in the middle of the floor. She was shaking from a seizure. Grayson stepped into the elevator, and the ghost faded.

He put a hand out, holding the door for her. "Ghosts just linger around all the time?"

She stepped into the confined area where the ghost no longer was. "Not exactly. It's only the ones who died in some traumatic way that linger. I used to think it was only those with unresolved issues, but I don't know anymore." With the list of things she hadn't been paying attention to and the different types of ghosts she ignored, she felt unsure about anything she thought she knew.

He pressed the button with a four on it, and the door closed. "I'm guessing hospitals aren't your favorite."

"No." She turned to him and blurted, "What's the deal with you repelling ghosts? Is that a Hunter thing?"

He shifted to face her. "I guess that would be something you'd notice. Yes, ghosts avoid Hunters. The theory is they get the same static itch around us that we get around demons. They don't like it. Demons have used that detail to hunt us in the past."

"Demons can see ghosts?" There was a whole history that wasn't just Hunters hunting witches and witches bonding with demons. There was a lot more going on than she understood.

"Some can. There are different breeds, classes, all with different abilities."

Vianna digested that. She knew that not all demons were strong enough to become familiars, and she knew summoning demons influenced spells. But this was so much more, an entire ecosystem of paranormal activity that witches were only a small part of. "What kind of demon is Shuck?"

He looked down at her, his eyes wide. "Did you just slip and finally give me his name, or am I getting somewhere with your trust?"

"I *don't* trust you." At least, she shouldn't. It wouldn't make sense with what he was and what she was.

"That's a shame." He took a step back and leaned against the railing on the wall. "I've been doing everything I can to earn it."

She'd noticed that too. But in her experience, trust equaled hurt and disappointment.

"So, Shuck, huh?" He gave a low whistle. "That's. . . something. Any Hunter worth their salt will know that name, but the traditional lore involves a large black dog with a strong streak of bloodlust. Rumor has it that if he takes to someone, there's no demon more loyal. Your Shuck is a house though."

"Now he is. He wasn't always in that form."

The elevator dinged, and the doors opened. Another hallway with more sage-green walls awaited them. She paused before broaching the fourth floor. There would be more ghosts, and it would be easier to do this with Grayson close by than face the multitude of them on her own.

She headed out of the elevator. "Come on, ghost repellent. Stay close."

17

Coven Mothers

Liam lay still in a thin bed with tubes running into his arms. A collection of monitors steadily beeped beside him. In the corner was a gray fabric chair where Ruby was curled into a ball, her head resting on the side and eyes shut. Even asleep, her face was red and blotchy from crying. A rumpled blanket slipped from her shoulder, and Vianna noticed she was still wearing the same hoodie from yesterday.

Grayson stepped into the room, scanning the bathroom and then the closet, where he even lifted the extra pillows stacked inside.

"I don't think they're hiding in the closet." She bit back a grin as she pulled out her phone.

"Never hurts to be sure."

Grayson did another once-over of the simple room while Vianna texted Tuck.

I'm here. Where are you?

"Liam?" Ruby sat up, rubbing her face with her hands as she tried to focus on them. She scrunched her face in recognition. "You're that fake witch and the cop."

Not exactly the best introduction Vianna had ever been given, but not the worst, either. "Vianna. And that's Grayson." Or maybe she should have introduced him as Detective Elliott. He nodded and didn't correct her, but he also didn't offer a reason for them being there. Vianna had been relying on Tuck for this part.

She twirled her thumb ring. "How's Liam?"

Ruby looked away, fidgeting with the blanket. "Doctors don't know when he'll wake up. *If* he'll wake up."

There was no good reply to that. Vianna didn't have siblings, but she understood caring about someone. And she understood feeling helpless to do anything.

Ruby tipped her chin up at Vianna. "I'm sorry about your eye. It looks like shit."

"It's fine." Vianna resisted touching it. It hadn't looked fine this morning in the mirror, but it would pass.

"I keep running through every minute down in that tunnel, trying to make sense of what happened." Ruby ran a hand through her hair.

"I get that," Vianna said. "I'm still trying to figure that out, too."

"James talked about you a lot. How you'd take us to the next level. How he'd been led to you. I thought it was all nonsense, but now I don't know. Not that it matters." Ruby took a deep breath and draped the blanket over the armrest. "As soon as Liam wakes up, I'm taking him home and we're never talking to James or any of you again."

Vianna didn't blame her. She fully understood the instinct to flee Salem.

Ruby stood, stretching her back. "You should watch out though. James already stopped by, and the little punk stole my phone and my equipment bag."

"Did you file a police report?" Grayson stood by the doorway.

Ruby rolled her eyes at him. "He can have it, the little prick. I'm out of whatever mental issue he has. I'm here with Liam until he wakes up, and then we're out of here."

"Why would he steal your phone?" Vianna wondered out loud. What was he up to?

"Because I wouldn't do what he wanted. He wanted me to call Ashley so he could go back into the tunnels. He didn't give two shits about Liam." Her voice squeaked on the last word.

Vianna really hoped Tuck got there soon, because she didn't know how to help them. "Ruby, I hate to ask this, but can you tell me why James latched on to the story of Elizabeth Derby West?"

"The museum exhibit." Ruby sighed. "The tunnels led us up into the museum, and James snuck inside to get something of Elizabeth's so that he could summon her. He was convinced it would be our big break if we aired the episode about Elizabeth when the museum exhibit opened."

So James had made the same connection as they had, just a whole lot sooner. And how had he known so early? At least one thing added up. The chain wrapped around the still-missing candle was probably stolen from the exhibit. It really was the trigger object.

"Did you see what happened to the candle James used? The one to call Elizabeth?"

"Haven't seen it since—" Ruby looked up at the ceiling and took a deep breath.

A *rap-rap* came from the door.

"I'm Dr. Dunford." A woman in a white coat with a frizzy ponytail stood by the door a couple feet from Grayson. "I performed Mr. Murphy's surgery. The nurse's station paged that the police needed information."

"I'm Detective Elliott." Grayson shook her hand. "I'm the one who called about a medical report for Mr. Murphy."

"Pleased to meet you." She handed over the folder she'd brought with her. "I ran the blood work you requested and did a visual check for botfly larvae. Negative on the larvae, but his blood work says he's got something going on with his liver, and we're giving him supplements to counter. Unless there's something else you want to share?" She looked over her glasses at Grayson.

Grayson held up the folder. "This should do it."

"Then if you'll excuse me, I have a surgery to get to."

"Thank you for your time," Grayson said as the doctor left.

Ruby stepped closer to Grayson. "What was that? I didn't give any permission for tests on my brother."

"Just part of the investigation. I'm not trying to cause any trouble," Grayson said. Vianna noticed how he moved the file behind his back to keep it safe.

"Investigation? That damn ghost again?" She pointed a finger at him. "No. We're not getting involved in this again. You two need to leave. And no more tests on Liam. No more anything. Leave us alone."

Grayson and Vianna backed out of the room and Ruby shut the door in their face.

"That didn't really go so well." Vianna looked up at Grayson.

He held up the folder. "But still productive. Where are you meeting Tuck?"

Vianna checked her phone and frowned at the message from Tuck.

Found something in the tunnels. Come see.

She texted back. *What about the hospital and supplies?*

Her phone vibrated right away. *Hospital later. Bring supplies.*

Okay? This was his idea, and bailing on the hospital was a disappointment. She'd gone through all the ghosts for nothing, and not just that, but she felt like Ruby and Liam really did need his help.

"When's Tuck getting here?" Grayson asked.

"I guess he's not." She tucked her phone back in her pocket. "Says he'll meet us at the tunnels, but I need to grab some stuff first. Plus, Dee should be off soon-ish. She'll want to come."

"I'll give you a ride home?" He lifted his brows in question. "Then meet you at the tunnels."

Vianna didn't argue, and they made a quick exit from the hospital, with Vianna noting again how the ghosts were repulsed by Grayson. Once inside his Chevy, he set the file beside him and started the truck, backing out of the parking spot.

"Botflies?" she asked.

He turned out of the parking lot and onto Main Street. "They show up sometimes beneath the skin during forced possessions."

"Gross." Vianna scrunched her nose. "And the liver. How'd you know?"

"I wondered if a demon-touched ghost had similar effects on a body as when it's forcefully possessed," he said. "The demon is like an infection, creating sores that create parasites, and the organs begin to shut down. It always starts with the liver."

It wasn't definitive proof that Elizabeth's ghost was demon-touched, but it was compelling. Vianna stared out the window, watching the business buildings blur into residential homes as she thought of demons and bondings, forced or chosen.

Her bonding with Shuck was willing. She didn't trust him, and she wasn't sure where they went from here, but she'd called for his help before they bonded and he'd given it. She'd gone to Mother's funeral and slipped into the legacy role. She'd made their bonding possible. And she hadn't made an effort to un-bond them since, if that was even possible. The thought made her feel sick to her stomach.

Grayson turned onto her street, and Vianna shook herself out of the stupor. "I'll text you when we head to the shop."

He pulled into her driveway. "Keep your cell on."

"You worried about a witch?"

"If you're driving *that*—" He nudged his chin toward her old Ford beside them. "—then yes."

"Hey." She narrowed her eyes. "That truck has been with me through everything. It's the most dependable thing in my life."

"Trucks don't last forever. Unless you're holding it together with rust-colored magic?"

Her reflection stared back from Grayson's sunglasses, and she wondered if she always looked that disheveled. She resisted taming her wavy hair. "No magic. Just good old grit and dirt." But magic wasn't a bad idea.

He chuckled. "If you say so."

She opened the truck door and hopped out.

He rolled down the window. "See you soon. Try not to get into too much trouble."

"Why does everyone say that?"

With a wave, he backed out of the driveway and drove off.

Vianna went inside the house and checked her phone, but there were no further messages from Tuck or anyone else. She hadn't even gotten a few feet away from the front door before a knock came. Maybe Grayson had forgotten something.

She reached back and opened the door. "Hey—" Oh. Not Grayson.

Ophelia's expression was firm, her muscles tightened in a pinched clench. "Are you okay?" Her afro had been twisted into locs at the ends that made her look fierce.

"Yes..." Vianna dragged out the single word, trying to catch up. The police escort and interrogation came back to her. "Oh! Yes, I'm fine. It was awkward and not something that will become a regular occurrence. But I'm fine."

"Come, then." Ophelia grabbed Vianna by the elbow and pulled her out the front door. "We've been waiting for you."

Vianna stumbled down the porch stairs, on the heels of Ophelia and her flowing skirts. "We? Who is 'we'?"

Ophelia didn't answer but instead pulled Vianna down the walkway and into Ophelia's front yard. They went up the porch steps and into her house before Vianna's elbow was finally freed.

Vianna froze in the entryway. The front door opened into a large common area with vaulted ceiling beams that housed a maze of branches. Although Ophelia's house looked to be two stories from the outside, the second story had no floor, but rather housed a tree-like playground for her bat familiar, Barnabus.

Alex Hall, mother to the Tidal Coven, and June Proctor, mother to the Mabon Coven, sat on a couch draped in a white knit lace cover. Ophelia busied herself at a serving table on the other side of the room.

There were small decorative tables around the room, all a shiny black that matched the wainscotting on the bottom half of all the walls. The top half of the walls were white and covered in white frames with pictures of Sixton witches and lots of photography of hands, dark-skinned and lighting candles, holding brooms, or holding other hands.

Ophelia turned from the serving table with an outstretched tea cup. "Drink, dear?"

Vianna raised her brow, looking from Ophelia to the other coven mothers. June had a dainty tea cup pinched between her thumb and pointer finger. She smiled sweetly with merlot-stained lips that matched her jumpsuit and took a sip from her cup. Alex had both hands clasped in her lap, no teacup to be seen around her. She wore leather pants with a satin blouse, and her new pixie haircut had sharp lines that matched her bone structure. When three of the four founding coven mothers met with you in secret, offering you tea, the outcome seemed obvious: you were dead.

Vianna crossed the room and took the outstretched cup. "Thank you."

The coven mothers stared at Vianna, not saying a word, waiting for her to drink the tea. It was a trust test. The urge to pull on her connection to Shuck was overwhelming. He knew so much more about the games played between witches and even other demons. She wanted his help, but if she opened the door to their connection, she would have to deal with his bloodlust. And for now, she didn't know if she could trust him. Vianna took a small sip of the tea. Cinnamon and orange.

"Now, then." Ophelia motioned to the green velvet chair beside the couch. "Have a seat."

Vianna sat as instructed, and Ophelia sat in a black throne-like chair across from them.

"We have been discussing your solitary status," Ophelia said.

That was not where Vianna had anticipated this conversation would go, and she was ready to save them a lot of time up front. "I'm not joining the OBC."

"Of course you're not." Alex flicked a wrist. "They're a mess. Zosia is going to have her hands full."

"Zosia?" Vianna asked.

"Yes," Ophelia said. "She'll be the next Original Blood mother."

She had assumed Tiphonie was the front runner for coven mother, but that was only because of Tiphonie's declarations. If she thought about it for half a second, Zosia was the obvious choice. Her line had never achieved mother status, but they were legacy and they'd been on the right hand of mothers for generations. It was a natural evolution for the coven.

"She's cleaning up the Barton mess as much as it can be," Alex said. "It was a strong move to display her control over Charles instead of hiding it away and acting like nothing happened."

"Yes, but we're here to discuss Vianna," Ophelia said.

"Indeed, we are," Alex said. "We had planned on a proper meeting and invitation for this discussion, but we were forced to move things up with what happened this morning. It was brazen of the police to come into *our* territory and cart off one of *our* prominent witches." Alex's expression was as rigid as her clipped tones.

Vianna tilted her head at *one of ours*.

"Oh, don't give us that look." Alex rolled her eyes. "You're an outcast, but you will always be one of *ours*. The Roots witches have been around since the beginning, and Shuck's display of power at the bonfire reminded everyone of just that fact. Solitary or not, Roots witches are not to be dismissed."

Vianna's breath stopped. She unpacked those words in her mind, and a sinking feeling weighed down her chest. Shuck's display had been about his bloodlust; she'd been sure of it. But now... now she felt very unsure.

"Which is why we think you should lead the solitary witches." Ophelia sipped her tea with a casualness that did not match her declaration.

Vianna stared, shocked. Her brain was shorting out because nothing in that statement made sense. "What?"

"Solitary numbers have swelled to an unprecedented amount," Ophelia continued.

"I still don't think we should count Google witches in their numbers," Alex grumbled. "They're not *real* witches."

"They're quite industrious," June chirped. "I find them fascinating."

"You find paint drying fascinating." Alex shook her head.

June pouted, but didn't argue.

"You'll represent solitary witches at coven mother meetings. You can keep them in line and update us on anything of relevance." Ophelia set down her cup on the table by her chair. "Insight on police movement and even the hoodoo community is also of interest."

"It seems you have your fingers in all of the pies." June grinned. "So smart. I love pie."

They wanted to use her the same way Grayson did. The coven mothers wanted an informant. It wouldn't work for a multitude of reasons, including the fact that Vianna trusted the coven mothers even less than she trusted Shuck. They wouldn't bat an eye to offer her up like a goat if it were to their benefit.

There was also the fact that the solitary witches weren't united; hence, their status title. "I wouldn't even know how to gather the solitary witches, much less represent them. And what if they don't want to be represented? Maybe they like the freedom of being unattainable."

"Oh, don't be so naive," Alex said. "It's annoying. Of course they want to be represented, because they want to be a part of our society, not fringe outcasts. And a long-standing, respected name like Roots—they'll be thrilled."

"Head home so you can think before speaking any more, Vianna. This is an important matter." Ophelia's tone was casual, but Vianna understood the weight of her words. There would be consequences if she said or did the wrong thing.

Vianna stood. A moment to think was a life raft she'd gladly latch on to. "Thank you for the tea."

She turned and made her way to the front door.

"And Vianna," Alex called after her. "Do tell the police that this was their one and only warning. If they drag another witch from her home, we'll return the favor—threefold."

Vianna looked over her shoulder. Ophelia and Alex had stern expressions, and June had an unsettling smile on her lips.

"Will do."

18

Not Friends

After verifying there was chaparral oil and myrrh gum in the conjure room, Vianna got in her Ford and headed to the cemetery nestled in the Salem Woods. She didn't give herself a moment to sit still or to think because she didn't know what to think. There was so much clambering around in her head that if she stopped to sort through it, she might drown. So she kept moving.

When she pulled into the gravel parking lot, she parked between Dee's orange Jeep and a white 4Runner she didn't recognize. The rain had calmed to a light misting, and the dirt was soft as she walked. The clouds were still dark and angry. Vianna pulled her hoodie up and headed beneath the weathered arbor, avoiding the overgrown poison ivy and scanning the grounds for Dee. She didn't see her.

A wispy hem of a dress slipped into Vianna's peripheral vision, then vanished. She sighed. "I know you're there, Helen."

The cemetery ghost floated from behind a tree, jaw hanging open to release her cringe-worthy scream. Vianna hunched her shoulders and turned away, heading toward the Roots plots on the other side of the field. The more distance she could put between Helen and her eardrums, the better.

She stopped at the edge of a grave: Victoria Roots, 1825—1907. Grandma Victoria was elusive, and Vianna had only seen her a time or two in the garden. Her grave plot boasted the thickest growth over the top of all the Roots witches.

Vianna let her backpack plop to the ground, then slid to her knees beside it. She'd brought an empty mason jar, and she scooped soft soil into it with her hand. With each scoop, she actively didn't think of Mother's grave just down the way or the recurring night-mare of being buried alive within said grave. Nor did she think of all the images Shuck had shown at the bonfire, all the killers with their various methods and preferences, their bodies here and feeding the life that had sprouted.

The pokeweed was easy to spot in the tangled mess of plants with its towering height and purple berries that drooped over the tombstone. She dug out the roots and used a pocket knife to cut away a chunk. A muffled sound made her pause, and she looked up, coming face-to-face with a pasty-white Grandma Victoria. She blew dust from her fingertips into Vianna's face.

A brown haze cocooned Vianna's head, and everything smelled of moldy cheese. She sucked in her breath, her body reacting before her mind to resist the toxins that were nothing more than a memory of long ago.

Grandma Victoria's face aged in some weird time warp. Youth faded as her skin sagged, then festered like it was being eaten by an infection, revealing decaying muscle and a thick white mucus that stretched out in strings. Something horrible had happened in her death. Vianna squeaked, yanking backward and squeezing her eyes shut.

After counting to ten and taking deep breaths, Vianna realized the soft, muffled sound hadn't faded. With a pinched expression of dread, she opened her eyes. Grandma Victoria was gone, and Vianna exhaled a breath of relief.

Not wanting to be snuck up on, she decided to investigate the noise. She stood, flicking clumps of mud from her jeans, and crossed to the circular building in the center of the field. The muffled sounds resembled crying, and Vianna hesitated. Slowly, she inched around the piles of small canvas bags that lined the perimeter of the maintenance building. Every legacy witch had a recipe for the best fertilizer. They left their super-secret bags of supplements for the groundskeepers to nourish the mini graveyard gardens during certain phases of the moon. Dee said they were the bane of her existence.

Vianna rounded the corner on a figure collapsed by a grave. "Tiph?"

Tiphonie straightened, wiping tears from her splotchy red cheeks. The tombstone beside her read Josephine Parker, and sprouts poked through the soil at the base.

"I didn't realize you were..." Vianna let her words trail off. She'd stumbled into an incredibly private moment that she had no business being a part of. "I heard something, and I—"

"I don't know what you're babbling about. I'm fine." Tiphonie smoothed out her hair and wiped below her eyes.

"Clearly," Vianna mumbled. She turned to leave, but Tiphonie's face was still puffy and red, making Vianna hesitate. "Are you okay?"

"Okay? Sure. Just peachy."

Vianna paused. Her tone made it clear that she was anything but peachy.

"Tomorrow is a big day for me, ya know." Tiphonie picked a blade of grass from the blanket she sat on, her legs folded to the side. She wore another variation of the politician's suit from Charles's speech, but this one was khaki.

Vianna put her hands in her pockets. "Can't say that I knew that."

"Of course you didn't, because you're a solitary. You wouldn't know *coven* business."

Sometimes the easiest way to communicate with Tiphonie was to not. Vianna started to leave, but Tiphonie kept talking.

"Tonight is *the* night. Charles is hosting a coven dinner at the museum so he can *propose* in front of everyone. And then tomorrow, there will be a vote for coven mother, which I was just informed I will lose. Coven mother status will leave the Parker line because of me, and I'll be left with... *Charles.*" Her bottom lip trembled for half a second before she sucked it behind her teeth and pushed her shoulders back into a more proper posture.

"Tiph." Vianna took a step closer. "It doesn't have to be this way."

"Don't." Tiphonie held up a hand and her eyes went glassy. "Don't act like we're friends."

Vianna groaned. "I'm not delusional."

Tiphonie's smile was more of a sneer. "You're supposed to offer full moon blessings for my impending *engagement.*"

"Since the title isn't official and you have plenty of time to pick your own future, I'll hold out."

Tiphonie barked out a laugh. "Tomorrow night will be the night I disappoint every witch before me. There's no future after that."

"Give it time. You'd be surprised how new paths can appear after the worst disaster. Better paths." Sometimes what was best was hidden away in options never seen.

"Must be nice," Tiphonie said. "Not caring about responsibility or honor. Just doing whatever flits your mood."

Deep breaths. Vianna would not snap at a daughter mourning her dead mother as her life crumbled around her.

"You wouldn't understand." Tiphonie dabbed at the stray tears on her cheeks. "You're too selfish to be coven-bound. You must give all of yourself to your coven to be worthy. Denying them anything is not an option. Coven mother or not, I'll do as they ask."

"Wow." Dee rounded the corner of the maintenance building, wearing her favorite pink rain boots. "It's all sunshine and cupcakes over here."

"No one asked *you*." Tiphonie glared at Dee.

"Lucky for me, I don't wait for others' permission to speak." Dee elbowed Vianna's ribs. "What's the schtick? What are you doing here? Everything okay?"

Vianna nodded. "Just picking up some supplies."

"I don't require company." Tiphonie folded her arms and pursed her lips. "You can both leave."

"Let's leave her be." Vianna nudged Dee toward the Roots graves. "How long has she been here?"

They were a few graves away before Dee answered. "About an hour. She's come almost every night since Josephine's funeral."

Tiphonie was truly mourning her mother, and Vianna couldn't imagine what that was like. But she could imagine the struggle in breaking tradition. No one deserved to be stuck with Charles, much less to be used as a pawn to feed the cash cow.

"Drove to a spot with service on my lunch break and did a little digging into the brothel ghosts." Dee pulled out some hard candies from her pocket and handed one over.

"Do tell." Vianna took the candy and ate it.

"More sad than anything." Dee stepped around a patch of white snakeroot. "There was a string of brothels set on fire in the name of religious purification not too long after Elizabeth's court date. There was a whole riot about cleaning up the seedy underbelly of Boston. I'm guessing our girls were caught in one."

That explained the fire death loop. "And Elizabeth was attached to them, so when she was awakened, she pulled them along with her."

"Makes sense to me. Elizabeth was a leper in the community after the divorce. She was shunned by everyone, even her own children.

It's not a big leap to assume that she would attach to the only women who had ever been there for her."

"And being solitary made her an easier target for an unwilling possession by a demon." Vianna rubbed at her chest and the ache within it.

Vianna was stronger with Dee, and every solitary witch out there would be stronger, safer, and be able to make more informed choices if there was a network where they could gain information.

Vianna stopped at Grandma Victoria's grave. "The founding coven mothers contacted me."

Dee pivoted toward Vianna. "What?"

"Yeah." Vianna scrunched her nose. "They want me to represent solitary witches."

Dee purposely dropped her jaw with exaggerated shock. "What does that even mean? What would you do?"

Vianna snorted. "Offer a blessing to Hades if I know. They mentioned regularly attending their meetings and not-so-casually mentioned updating them on police and hoodoo affairs."

"Oooh... double agent." Dee fiddled with the plastic bag until she found the right color of candy. "I'd be down to have you represent me."

"You're biased. I'm not so sure other solitary witches would take me seriously, but the mothers felt Shuck's fire display handled that."

"Obviously." Dee shrugged her shoulders. "Why else would he have done it?"

Vianna stiffened. "Because he loves murder and misses it. A declaration of his intentions."

Dee tilted her chin down, staring hard at Vianna. "You're joking, right?"

"He's bonded with eleven generations of murderers. Of course I'm not joking. You can't possibly think he doesn't want to kill again. Doesn't want me to kill for him." Vianna's words came out in a rush.

"Vie." Dee groaned. "You really need to figure out this whole trust issue."

"What?" Vianna gasped. "What does trust have to do with anything?"

Dee pursed her lips, clearly not wanting to have this conversation. Vianna folded her arms over her chest, waiting.

"Fine." Dee's voice was soft. "You assume the worst in everyone. Even me."

"I do not assume the worst in you," Vianna argued.

"Oh yeah? And when you found out I was researching your heritage, did you trust that I was doing it to help you? Or did you automatically assume I was doing something to hurt you?"

Vianna clamped her mouth shut. She wanted to pace, wanted to throw something. Why was everything suddenly so hard? "I don't think you intentionally want to hurt me."

"Right. You just think I'm unable to understand the perimeters of my own actions and will blindly and dumbly hurt you because of it." Dee put a hand on her hip.

With a big exhale, Vianna released her balled fists, hanging at her side. "It sounds really bad when you put it like that."

Dee nodded with an unamused expression. "And you think that Shuck—what—doesn't know you after watching your entire childhood? Come on, Vie. He knows you won't kill, and yet, he *chose* to bond with you. You know demons don't stay with the same line, often because they don't like the next witch in line. They're prickly little pricks, and it's a choice on both sides. I highly doubt he went into your bonding with intentions of changing you. Not bonding with you would have been way easier."

Vianna felt awful, like a weight was pressing her down. A weight of her own doing. Not everyone should be trusted—in fact, most shouldn't—but not everyone should be treated like the enemy either. She wanted Dee in her life. She even wanted Shuck in her life.

Sorting through all the witch and demon drama without him the past two days had sucked. "I'm sorry. I'm not good at... people-ing. Or whatever. I'll work on trusting."

"That would be nice." Dee pulled Vianna into a large hug. "I love you. We'll figure it out."

Vianna hugged her back. "Love you, too." She was going to have to talk to Shuck, and she didn't know where to begin.

Dee pulled back and picked up Vianna's backpack, handing it over. Vianna put it on, and they started walking toward the parking lot.

"Okay." Dee rubbed her hands together. "I want you to keep an open mind."

Keep an open mind was never something anyone said before good news. "Out with it."

"You ready?" Dee grinned ear to ear. "Broomstix Bitches!"

She couldn't be serious, but she looked serious, so Vianna did her best not to laugh. "Let's pin that one as a *maybe*."

"Maybe? That's *the* name! It's short, snappy, fun, and you can never go wrong with alliteration."

"Huh." Vianna chuckled. "You're about to get off, right? Tuck asked us to swing by the tunnels. I got a weird text about showing us something."

"I'm off in thirty minutes," Dee said. "And don't think I didn't notice the subject change."

Vianna grinned and headed toward the truck as Dee stopped at the gate. "See you at home."

"And don't cancel out Broomstix Bitches yet," Dee called to Vianna's back. "Give it a chance!"

19

Proper Protocol

Vianna sat in her Ford parked in the driveway, ignoring the swaying form of Grandma Susannah in her peripheral vision. Grandma was replaying her death loop, the branch making its familiar creak as the hem of her dress swooshed backward, then forward. Vianna tried to focus on sorting out how she felt about Shuck and how to communicate with him. The first step was to stop shutting down their connection when he did something that freaked her out. That hadn't helped anything.

She could see the imaginary door she'd created in her mind, made of thick wood with a brass doorknob and hinges. The brass had grown, stretching over the wood in twining designs as though magic had crept over her own imaginary creation. Perhaps it had. It was time to stop running from him. Now or never.

With a quick mental shove, the fancy door flung open, and she waited for the onslaught of whatever came next. Nothing happened.

Of course nothing happened, because she had no idea what she was doing or how any of this worked. With a grumble, she got out of the truck and jogged up the porch stairs. The front door to the house didn't open on its own, but it wasn't locked either.

When she pushed the door open, a broom fell forward, and she lurched to catch it, barely saving it before it hit the ground. It was the broom from Tuck that Shuck loved to be swept with. Was Shuck moving the broom, or was the broom moving itself? She held it out for examination, eyes narrowed and considering, but only saw an old-fashioned broom.

She looked up at the staircase, then across to the living room. "Fine. I'll sweep while we talk."

She dropped her backpack on the bottom stair and flipped the bristle side of the broom down. "I'm holding on to the no-killing rule."

She swept around the perimeter of the living room. "But I'll try to stop assuming that you want to break me in order to change that rule. Because that's not changeable and we chose each other. And I'll stop running. No more shutting the door."

She worked her way into the kitchen but felt no response from Shuck, no rumbles within her bones, no movement within the house, just the scrap of bristles against hard wood as though he were just a house. Disappointment pulled at her insides, and she didn't know what to do next.

Lights shot across the bay windows, and Dee pulled into the driveway with her Jeep.

Vianna stored the broom back in the pantry, bristle up. She missed his growl-purring.

The front door clicked open, and then the third stair creaked as Dee ran up them. "I hurried, but I had to wait for Tiph to finish up. Give me five minutes to change!"

Vianna moved into the living room and grabbed her backpack. She had the graveyard dirt, a pouch of myrrh gum, and a vial of chaparral oil. She added the pokeweed root sack from her pocket.

Flashlights would help if Shuck wasn't going to speak with her, so she went to the linen closet and loaded up on several supplies. With Tuck's help, they would find the candle and destroy it. Then all of this would be over. If they got rid of Elizabeth, the brothel ghosts should go too. Hopefully.

Vianna considered wearing the talisman in order to bring the grandmas, but adding more ghosts to the mix sounded more like chaos than help. Plus, she wasn't sure how that worked with Grayson there. Grandma had kept her distance when he was here, but she hadn't completely disappeared. Same with the ghosts in the tunnels. Maybe it was the weaker ghosts who left entirely. She pulled out her phone and texted him about heading to the shop, just like she'd promised. See, she could trust and communicate.

Dee rounded the corner from the stairs, her leather potion belt slung over a black jumpsuit with cheetah-print ballet flats. The large yellow and orange wrist bangles clanked with each shift of her arm.

"No army print?" Vianna grinned.

"In the wash. I should get more." Dee dangled her keys. "I'm driving."

* * *

The drive took twenty minutes longer than usual thanks to the traffic jam downtown by the museum. Vianna figured it was the coven dinner and wedding proposal Tiphonie had mentioned. The entire coven must have come out with the traffic. Vianna texted Tuck to let him know they were coming, but he didn't reply.

Dee parked in a side alley. There was no sign of Grayson's shiny blue Chevy, but when they turned the corner out of the alley, he was waiting on the sidewalk just outside the shop.

He pointed at a sign taped to the door. "Says closed for inventory."

"Inventory?" Vianna repeated. "Probably a ruse until he handles the tunnels and Ashley." She peered through the display window but saw no movement.

"The side door jiggled open, and I did a sweep," Grayson said. "The shop is empty."

"Aren't you supposed to wait for backup in a situation like that?" Dee peeked through the shop window with her hands cupped around her eyes.

A small group of tourists with to-go cups from the coffee shop down the street walked by, giving them the side-eye at first. But then they kept walking.

"If it seemed dangerous—" Grayson headed around the corner of the building. "—I would have called in backup other than you two. No offense."

"It's a little offensive," Dee mumbled as they left the window to follow him.

"There's no one in the shop. They either stepped out or went into the tunnels. And the PD isn't going to know what to do with a ghost, so I held off on calling them."

The side door that Grayson had propped open led into the back of Tuck's hoodoo shop.

Vianna grimaced. "You realize this lock is so crappy because no one in their right mind would break into a hoodoo shop, right? We'll probably get a rash in our armpits and between our toes or something."

"That would piss me off." Grayson ducked to avoid a hanging ring of dried chicken claws. "If he's in the tunnels, he's in danger. We'll have to take the risk."

Nothing looked out of place. There was a stack of bricks in the corner that hadn't been put onto the shelves yet, and Tuck's herb racks that hung from the ceiling were a little more sparse than usual, but that wasn't exactly some great sign of trouble.

They moved into the hallway with Grayson in the lead and

Dee trailing behind. Grayson paused at the linen closet across from Tuck's gaming room. He blocked the doorframe, and Dee poked over his right shoulder on her tiptoes while Vianna peeked around his left side. There was no sign of a struggle or anything amiss, but the trapdoor was open.

"Do you smell that?" Dee shifted around Grayson to get in the closet.

Vianna sniffed, tilting her head and closing her eyes as she tried to identify the herb that lingered in the air. It was earthy with a touch of celery and pepper. She opened her eyes to Grayson's warm gaze. Her cheeks heated, and she tucked a strand of hair behind her ear.

"Herbs. Angelica root again for sure. Something else too."

"Sulfur?" Dee asked.

Grayson poked around the pantry, looking between folded blankets and behind monitors. "I smell the sulfur too. A lot of demons can give off that smell."

"It's also pretty common in some hoodoo wards," Vianna said.

She bent down and dabbed her finger into a red dust that marked the floor. She lifted her finger to her nose. That was the source of the sulfur.

"Tuck was up to something." Dee looked into the black hole that led to the tunnels.

"If he went down there by himself, he might be in trouble." Vianna shifted the backpack on her shoulders. Facing Elizabeth or the brothel ghosts made her fidgety, but she wouldn't leave Tuck and Ashley on their own.

"Hold up." Grayson scooted Dee over and took a small flashlight from his pocket, then shined it into the tunnels. "You can't just go barging into places. I didn't clear the tunnels."

"I wasn't barging." Dee looked over his shoulder and down below.

"You already said the cops can't handle ghosts. That's our territory. You know you need us."

Vianna made her move while they were bickering, lowering herself down the ladder. If Tuck was dealing with Elizabeth, she didn't want him doing it on his own. Was that what he wanted to show her? Why couldn't he have waited?

"That's not how this works," Grayson growled at Vianna as he climbed down after her. "We're going over protocols after this. You *never* go first. Always wait for me to clear the area."

He climbed down next, whipping out his flashlight to search the cavern as Dee climbed down. Vianna pulled more flashlights from her backpack and handed one to Dee.

"It's naive to speak in absolutes." Dee swung a light beam around the cavern.

"Focus, guys. We're looking for Tuck." Vianna didn't see anything in the main cavern. "Tuck?" Instead of a reply, her own voice echoed between the tunnel walls.

From what she could remember, the broken furniture and torn boxes all looked to be in the same spots. Dee would know for sure with her photogenic memory. Vianna took a steadying breath. There was no frigid temperature drop or rose oil in the air. That was something.

Her flashlight beam roamed over black tennis shoes sticking out from behind a dresser, and she paused. Her heart rate jumped. The upturned black soles were covered in painted-on symbols. Someone was unconscious on the floor, someone wearing the same shoes Tuck always wore. Vianna couldn't move, staring at the red painted squiggles, arrows, and twirls.

Her blood felt like slush clogging her veins, and she wasn't sure if an army of ghosts were incoming or if her own terror had turned her insides to ice. She forced herself to take another step forward. She didn't want what she saw to be real. It was someone else. Something else. Or maybe nothing. Could it be nothing? Her voice came out in a whisper. "Tuck?"

Grayson and Dee rushed forward from behind, and she knew she needed to move. Faster. Tuck needed help. Her movements felt like slow motion, slowed down because of the slush in her veins.

"Help me move this dresser." Grayson nodded to Dee.

They lifted it together, revealing an unconscious and motionless Tuck. The cold fear inside of Vianna heated to anger, and she jolted into action. Dee slid to her knees at his side, and Vianna stood over them both. Dried blood crusted down the side of his head and over his eyebrow piercing. He was still, too still.

She should have gotten there sooner. She should have never gone to the cemetery, but straight to the tunnels when he didn't show at the hospital. She should have told Tuck more about Elizabeth and the danger she posed.

Dee pulled her hand back from his chest. "He's breathing."

Vianna fished out the first aid kit from her backpack and opened it up. Dee yanked up Tuck's t-shirt. There was no bruising or swelling.

"I didn't get a look at Liam's chest. Were there any marks?" Dee asked.

"I got a look, but no marks." Grayson leaned down, fingers on Tuck's throat to check his pulse. "His pulse is strong though, stronger than Liam's was."

It didn't prove his heart was okay, or even his liver, but it was something. Dee pulled vials from her leather potion belt, mixing and shaking. Vianna handed over a square of cotton and Dee soaked it with a dark blue bottle and waved it under Tuck's nose. Vianna held her breath. He had to wake up. He couldn't lay there, unmoving, like Liam.

After a few moments, Tuck's eyes flew open. Vianna let out a loud exhale. He pushed into a sitting position, then grabbed the side of his head with a groan.

"That asshole," he growled.

"You'll have to be more specific. I know a lot of those." Dee gave a nervous laugh and pushed his hand away to look at his head. "Let me bandage that."

Tuck puckered his mouth but didn't argue. Vianna handed the first aid kit over to Dee. Tuck's eyes tracked the cavern, landing on Vianna and Grayson. "Where's Ashley?"

"We haven't seen her," Grayson said. "Shop is empty too. What happened?"

Tuck's shoulders tensed. "We need to find her before that whacko does something stupid." He swatted Dee's hand away and pushed up to his feet with a slight wobble.

"Take it easy, Tuck." Grayson stepped forward.

Tuck shook his head. "I'm fine. We need to find Ashley. James took her."

20

You've Got This All Wrong

"James?" Vianna repeated. She'd been so concerned about Elizabeth, she hadn't considered James.

"Walk us through what happened," Grayson said.

Tuck put a hand against the dresser to steady himself. "You were here earlier. With the police."

"He's the cop I mentioned. Grayson." *The cop* was a bit vague for an introduction, but she didn't know what else to call him.

Tuck bent and picked up a chunk of jagged rock, the corner stained with blood. "He snuck up on me from behind. Little punk." He tossed the rock back down.

"Have you been down here this whole time? Since you texted?" Vianna asked.

"What are you talking about?" Tuck felt his front and back pockets, then rubbed his chin as he looked at the surrounding dirt. "I haven't texted since we spoke about meeting at the hospital." He threw his hands in the air. "My phone is gone. Keys too."

"James used his phone to text you," Dee said.

Tuck clenched his fist. "He must have Ashley's phone too. She texted me to come down into the tunnels."

"Footsteps lead further into the tunnels." Grayson pointed to the dirt floor. "Only one set though," he said, still studying the prints. "If Ashley is with James, she's being carried."

Tuck's face flexed into a hard grimace. "I should have known better. I charged down here without a plan or a weapon. Ashley would never come down here on her own."

Grayson bent down and picked up a piece of trash by the rock wall. "Duct tape. Let's get moving." He stood and unbuttoned his holster but didn't pull the gun.

"One sec." Tuck turned to Vianna. "Did you bring the stuff I asked for? If James is using ghosts, we need to be ready."

"Yeah." Vianna pulled the backpack from her shoulders and pulled out the glass jar, handing it over.

When she handed over the myrrh gum, he stopped her. "Chew on it first."

Vianna frowned but put the soft rock in her mouth and chewed gently. It had a bitter, pungent taste, but she didn't complain. Tuck unscrewed the mason jar and dumped in the pokeweed root and then the chaparral oil. He held out the jar for her to spit in the myrrh gum. Once it was all combined, he screwed on the lid and handed it back.

"Shake it up. When we find the candle, douse it. I'm betting James has it." Tuck pulled his vape from his pocket and inhaled. When he exhaled, the smoke smelled sweet.

"You're vaping herbs?" Dee asked. "For protection?"

"Sure," Tuck said. "Among other things."

"Let's do this." Dee looped arms with Vianna, and she noticed the slight tremor. Vianna was scared too. Not of James, but of Elizabeth.

Grayson took the lead, sweeping each tunnel and cavern with his flashlight beam. Tuck brought up the rear, muttering words Vianna couldn't decipher through puffs of smoke that smelled of angelica root and something sugary. Vianna looked for ghosts, but each cavern contained nothing more than piles of forgotten furniture and layers of cobwebs, until they stepped into the cavern where they'd first met Elizabeth.

A light draft of rose oil lingered. Everyone slowed, looking to Vianna. She turned in a circle, twice, making sure she didn't miss anything. "No ghosts."

They pushed deeper into the tunnels. The further they went, the tighter the tunnels shrank, and the group shifted into a single line. They hadn't gone this far into the tunnels before. The air grew heavy with humidity, and Vianna resisted the urge to brush off phantom spider webs from her neck and arms every other minute.

At the end of the narrow corridor was an antique door that looked straight out of a castle. A section of a portcullis was bolted to the oiled wood and the handle and hinges were made of thick iron.

"There are more fresh tracks through here." Grayson reached for the ornately curved handle, but it didn't budge. He fished out a small metal pin from somewhere. "Shine the light on the lock so I can see."

"You're like a military Mary Poppins." Dee's voice shook despite her words.

Vianna squeezed Dee's arm, then let go in order to angle her beam into the lock mechanism so Grayson could see better. His hands were steady and sure as he tilted his head to the side, listening to the scrape of metal against the inside of the lock.

Something bumped against the toe of Vianna's boot, and she looked down just as Grayson bolted up and away from the door. On instinct, Vianna jumped back too, widening her eyes in search of the unknown danger.

Grayson shook his large shoulders. "Rats."

"We're in underground tunnels." Vianna sucked in her lips to keep from chuckling. Some of her nerves eased away at the simple reaction to something predictable and normal. "Rats are a given."

Grayson knelt back down on one knee, focusing on the lock. "That's classified intel."

Vianna kept the light on the lock but repeatedly looked over her shoulder, checking for Elizabeth or any other ghost that might sneak up on them. Tuck glanced back with her in reaction each time.

The lock clicked, but Grayson waited to open the door, holding a finger in the air to warn everyone. He motioned for all of them to back up against the wall before he pulled his gun. Dee squished close to Vianna, crushing her hand in an iron grip.

The tunnel was narrow, and they crammed against each other with nowhere to move or get out of the way if something charged at them. Something like a raging demon-ghost. But there was no backing out now. Elizabeth had to be dealt with. James had to be controlled, and they needed to make sure Ashley was okay.

Grayson turned the knob and shoved the door back.

Vianna sucked in her breath.

But nothing happened. Nothing rushed at them through the open doorway. There was no shouting, no tortured screaming, nothing. Grayson went in first, then the rest of them slinked in around the stone wall. The cavern was enormous, three times the size of the others and three times as tall too. Low-watt light bulbs lit up the corners, casting an eerie glow over the cracks that stretched across the walls.

"Chickaboo," a husky voice sang.

Vianna turned to find her poetry girlfriend perched on a stack of wooden crates with her long braid draped over her shoulder. A stocking had slipped down her knee, and she dangled a glass bottle from her fingers. She made a kissy face before taking a swig from her bottle.

More brothel ghosts were sprawled over countless crates stacked in piles against the walls. Tables covered in stacks of paper took over the center of the cavern. Everyone looked to Vianna again before spreading out. She swallowed the lump in her throat. "There are ghosts, but no Elizabeth. Her entourage."

"She can't be too far behind, then." Dee didn't leave Vianna's side but looked up and around. "I think we're beneath the museum. Looks like a storage area. There are even vaults."

"Explains the doors and why they're locked." Grayson was doing his military thing, peeking around corners and behind stacks of boxes.

"And the gaudy junk instead of broken furniture." Dee pointed at a painting of a warship with an ornate gold frame as they moved further into the opening.

"Found her! Over here." Grayson holstered his gun and pushed back a sliding door of metal bars that half hid a secluded enclave to reveal a body lying still in the dirt.

All three of them rushed to where Grayson stood. Tuck pushed past them.

"Ashley!" He wedged between a stack of crates, knocking over the top one and spilling a wave of packing peanuts into the air. Then he knelt beside her, and a faint whimper responded. Her eyes fluttered open, and Tuck gently worked off the duct tape that stretched across her swollen face. She struggled to wake up, leaning into Tuck as she tried to sit up.

Ashley had been knocked out and stuffed into a vault of sorts, a really large one. A sliding wall of metal bars that, when closed, secured the area and everything in it. A creak echoed in the high rock ceilings, and Vianna turned. To the right and outside of the vault area, a set of stone stairs stretched up to another ancient door that swung open. Gold coins clattered down the stairs, and James stumbled down a step, belatedly trying to catch the fallen coins while still clinging to the handful in his flipped-up t-shirt.

"Vianna!" His crooked smile took over his narrow face. "Finally! I've been waiting for you."

Everyone went still, staring.

James took everyone in, from Tuck and Ashley on the ground to Grayson beside them, and ending on Dee, who still clung to Vianna's arm. His grin slid away as his eyes jumped to Vianna. "What are *they* doing here? They have no skills for ghost hunting. No. We don't need them. This was just supposed to be you and me."

Awkward silence hung in the air, the kind where Vianna thought she should move or do something but had no idea what. "You and me?"

Dee straightened, releasing Vianna's arm and inching in front of her. "Is this all about Vie? Are you obsessed with her?"

"What?" James blurted. "No."

"It's okay." Dee put up her palms in surrender, becoming more herself. James didn't quite scare her like Elizabeth did. "No judgment here."

"It's not like that." James bent and picked up some of the coins, adding them to the growing pile in his shirt pouch.

"Keep your hands where I can see them, James. Slowly come down the stairs." Grayson had his hand on his holster, inching in front of Ashley as Tuck finished cutting away the rest of the duct tape.

"My hands are full, man." James stopped two stairs from the bottom, lifting his pouch of coins and making them clank against each other.

Vianna backed away, away from the others, pulling Dee with her. Maybe she could distract him from Ashley so Tuck could get her out of here. The three groups formed a triangle with James at the point on the stairs.

"Go ahead and put the coins down." Grayson's tone was firm but not raised. "I have to take you in for questioning about Ashley."

"You've got this all wrong." James shook his head, and greasy strands of hair flopped into his eyes. "I'm here to help. Vie and I can handle the ghost. The show is gonna take off. We'll be famous."

"You're crazy." Ashley was awake now, visibly shaking, her arms wrapped around herself. She'd gotten to her feet, but stayed behind Grayson. "You pretended to be Ruby and lured me down here and then used me as a hostage!"

"What? Hostage? No." James looked aghast, shaking his head. "You wouldn't have responded to a text from *me*. I needed access to the tunnels. What else was I supposed to do? Then you freaked out about using Ruby's phone, and I didn't want you to run to the cops. Vie and I just need one night to film. I was going to untie you as soon as we were done. You were being *irrational*."

"James," Grayson said. "Focus on me. Turn around and get on your knees with your hands behind your back. I have to take you in so we can clear all of this up."

"You're messing everything up," he hissed at Grayson, spraying spit as he spoke. He marched down the remaining two stairs.

"Stay right there. On your knees." Grayson took a step back, his hawk eyes tracking every movement James made. His hand remained on his gun as he positioned his body to block both Ashley and Tuck.

James leaped forward, flinging the coins in his shirt at Grayson as he pulled a gun from his waistband. James slammed the vault door shut as a gun went off. Dee grabbed Vianna, and they dove behind a table. The gunshot carried on as it bounced between the rocks and Vianna hunched forward with her hands on her ears. Rats darted from between crates.

Dee was on the ground by Vianna. James howled like a cat in heat, and Vianna peeked from behind a wooden box, but everything felt jumbled. She stumbled toward the mini-vault area that was now closed off like a jail. Hands grabbed her from behind, and the smell of canned bacon wrapped around her.

Metal pressed against her temple, and the hand around her middle tightened.

"Slide your gun over." James's breath was hot against her ear from behind.

Grayson stood behind the bars, chest rising and falling in deep breaths. Then Vianna heard Ashley whimper behind him, crumpled in the dirt. Tuck knelt at her side as he pulled off his t-shirt to hold against the blood on her abdomen. She'd been shot. And now James was shoving the still-warm muzzle of the same gun into the side of Vianna's head.

"Slide your gun over. Now!" James screamed in a shrill tone.

21

Xanadu

Grayson's jaw flexed, and his eyes narrowed on Vianna.

James shoved the end of his gun hard against her temple, making her stumble. Her heart raced as she tried to think of every option. She could stomp his foot—that was a thing in movies—and then Grayson could shoot him while she dove in the other direction. She exhaled a long breath to steady her heart and mind. That option didn't feel as practical with a gun barrel pressed flush against her head and Ashley bleeding out in the corner.

Grayson knelt low to the ground. His thumb flicked the safety as he placed his gun in the dirt outside the bars and shoved it toward them. James released Vianna instantly, scrambling toward the gun and scooping it up. Dee rushed to Vianna and pulled her backward.

James remained in the center of the cavern, clutching his arm to his side and yowling. He'd been shot when Ashley was shot. The echo had been two gunshots. A large blood stain spread over his shoulder.

Grayson moved to the prison bars that locked him, Tuck, and

Ashley together in the vault and pulled. They didn't budge. "James, open this door *now*. If you do, I can still help you."

"*You're lying*," James squealed. "You won't help me—you're the one who shot me!" His voice was high, and his words ran on top of each other.

"It was a nonfatal shot. You'll be fine. Put pressure on it." Grayson moved to the other side of the vault and tugged on the bars. Nothing. "James, open this damn door."

"I'm not *fine*." James sounded on the verge of tears. He pointed the gun in his hand at Dee. "Help me."

He shook the gun to emphasize the command. Her face had a deathly pallor.

"James! The door," Grayson growled. "*I* can help you."

"I don't know how!" James yelled, waving the gun through the air. Everyone flinched.

"Enough with the gun." Vianna's heart pounded. He could just as easily shoot someone else by accident. He seemed to have about as much firearm training as she did, which was none.

"I'm helping, all right?" Dee's voice wavered, but she walked over to James. "You don't need the gun."

Vianna slipped off her backpack and pulled out the first aid kit, handing it to Dee.

"I could use something to stop the bleeding over here," Tuck shouted. "Ash isn't doing well. Open the door, James!"

Grayson had his phone out. "No service down here. Come on, James. Don't let someone die."

"This isn't my fault," James whined. "Why does no one understand?"

James was unraveling, and yelling at him was only making it worse. They needed to calm him down. Vianna needed to distract him enough to talk him out of that gun.

"I know." Vianna's voice cracked, and she cleared her throat. "This is all a misunderstanding. But you need to let everyone go so we can clear it up."

James whimpered. "No. Then everything is for nothing. We're filming the episode. You'll see. This will all be worth it."

Dee tentatively approached James and opened the first aid kit. She held up oversized tea bags for James to see. "Witch hazel and yarrow. Can I give this to them to help her bleeding? Ashley was shot too."

"Fine." James raised his chin at Vianna. "You do it."

Vianna gathered the tea bags then walked over to the bars, passing them off to Grayson. "Is she gonna be okay?" There was a lot of blood soaked through Tuck's shirt.

"She needs help now." Grayson's expression was grim as he took the herbs. He spoke with his voice low. "If you can distract him, I can get them out of here."

Distract him. Her heart raced. He didn't want to shoot her—he wanted to film a stupid show. She could do that. She clenched her hands into fists to stop the shaking. There was no time to freeze up or waver.

Grayson raised his voice. "James, you need to put the gun down and go get help."

James shook his head, his lips pressed together, then spoke. "Not until this is done. There's always the darkest hour in every episode, in every *real* ghost hunt." His breathing was heavy. "The point where everyone is scared and they want to call it quits. It's the shows that push through, that keep filming—that's when the good stuff happens. We're doing this. We're going to be famous."

Dee finished his bandage and James scrambled to his feet, aiming his gun at Vianna. "This can still work."

"James." Grayson's voice was low. "She'll do what you want without the gun. Put it away. What do you need?"

James didn't put the gun down. "Draw a circle. We're summoning Elizabeth." He waved the gun at Dee. "You. Go turn on the cameras."

Three different tripods were tucked between stacks of crates in different areas of the cavern. Dee handed a pouch of salt to Vianna from her potions belt, then moved to the cameras. Vianna glanced at Grayson trapped behind the bars. *Distract him.* She could do this. Up the stairs and into the museum was the closest help, but as long as James had a gun on them, they had to play his game before they could do anything else.

"What's the plan, James? After we summon her?" Vianna walked in a slow, large circle as she poured pink salt.

"That's up to Elizabeth. Maybe she just needs someone to hear her story before she can be at peace. Maybe she has a secret she needs to tell us. Or maybe the necklace I found is tied to some important moment. I wrapped it around your candle." He grinned, proud of his innovation.

"I know this is new for you, but I've watched you, and you're going to be a natural. You'll see. We can do it together." James nodded to himself, as if it all made perfect sense. He'd pressed the handle of the gun against his wound, like he was stopping the bleeding with pressure but forgot his hands were full.

If Vianna could fake-summon Elizabeth and say the ghost wanted them in the museum, that would make James agree to going upstairs, and upstairs there would be help and phones that would work. Someone to call who could help Ashley.

Vianna tried to remember what the newspaper had said about the Derby exhibit. She needed a reason why Elizabeth would want them upstairs. They had Derby West items on display, recreating famous rooms from her house. She'd need details from Dee's iron-clad memory. But it could work.

"You're sure I can do this, James?" Vianna kept her voice soft to appear non threatening.

James gave a tentative smile back. "I know you can. And after we summon Elizabeth, we can summon others using objects from the museum. I grabbed the gold coins from the Black beard exhibit. We're gonna hit so big. You'll see." He looked at each blinking red light from the cameras. "Don't block those, Dee. Stay to the right a little more. And Vie, when you face the camera, don't squint at the light. It looks amateur."

"Actually, it would be easier with Dee's help." Vianna focused on the ground as she finished with the salt. Two against one was better odds. She needed Dee.

"Can she see them too?" James paused in his pacing.

After a minute, Dee stepped forward, wringing her hands. "No. But I'm expert-trained in summoning. Covens hire me all the time." Dee raised her chin.

Bless the goddess for everything Dee in Vianna's life. She was playing along, despite the gun being waved at her face.

James pouted his lips and then must have decided he believed her because he nodded, waving her over. "Yeah. All right. The whole witch thing, right? Ya know, it might even add something different to the show. Set us apart, showing how *real* witches work." He nodded again. He did that a lot, agreeing with himself.

James kept the gun pointed at them as he inched backward to a black duffel bag. He looped his good arm with the gun through the strap and tossed it to Dee. "The candle is in there."

Dee knelt and unzipped the bag, shuffling around until she pulled out the candle with the thin chain wrapped around the base. She stepped into the circle and placed the candle in the center. Vianna leaned down and doodled meaningless symbols into the dirt with her finger. Dee hunkered next to her.

"Don't forget this one." She traced a looping circle into the dirt. It was all meaningless, but James wouldn't know that.

Vianna whispered as she traced more looping circles. "The museum display. I can't remember it."

Not giving James a chance to get suspicious, she quickly stood, which also didn't give Dee a chance to answer. But Dee was clicking her nails together, her thinking tell. She knew what Vianna needed and was recalling the article.

Vianna stood over the candle with her hands out, palms up. She reached through the open connection to Shuck. *Stay still*, she pleaded. *I know I opened our connection, but not now. Do not help. No magic.* She wasn't even sure if he was paying attention or willing to work with her at all anymore. That problem was for later.

"By the power of north, south, east, and west, I call upon the forgotten ghost of Elizabeth Derby West." There was no power of four directional hexagons on their own. She'd have to call a demon from each to make it matter, and she didn't need four. But all of it sounded good, she hoped.

Dee gripped Vianna's clammy hand, and she shakily outstretched her other. "Under the authority of the goddess Xanadu, I give you protection to join us."

Vianna sucked in her lips, biting back a smirk at Xanadu. They could do this. They were trembling and terrified, but they could still do this.

"You forgot the most important part." James stumbled forward and bent down, quickly lighting the candle. Vianna didn't realize what he was doing until it was too late.

An icy breeze washed through the cavern. The brothel ghosts suddenly woke, clambering off the crates, and moved closer to the circle. *No, no, no.* This wasn't supposed to be working; she hadn't lit the candle. Then Vianna looked down and saw the dancing flame. The ghost of Elizabeth Derby West with her frizzy halo of hair appeared outside the circle.

"Fuck," Vianna said.

"Fuck?" Dee repeated. "That's not a part of the plan."

Elizabeth Derby West had the darkest, blackest pit of eyes Vianna had ever seen. Her fitted nightgown gathered around the chest, then flowed out and to her ankles like rolling fog.

"Vie," Dee whispered loudly.

This was not good. "It worked," Vianna croaked. The ghost wasn't strong enough for the others to see, not without consuming other ghosts.

"It's okay." It was. It was fine. She could still say Elizabeth needed them to go upstairs to the display. They could still get help for Ashley and then smash the candle and necklace to bits. This could still work.

"Ask her what she's looking for." James knelt just outside the circle, pressing his arm with the hurt shoulder into his chest.

Perfect. Vianna took a breath and asked, "We want to help. No one here wants to hurt you. How can we help you find peace?"

Elizabeth hovered in front of them, and the brothel ghosts began to stumble closer. They needed to hurry.

"Do you hear that?" Dee gripped Vianna's arm and swayed like a damsel. "There's whisperings. So much anger."

James cocked his head as though he might be able to hear something. The gun hung at his side instead of him waving it around like a toddler. That was improvement.

"What was that? You want to be buried with your duvet?" Dee spoke to empty air, nowhere near the direction where ghost-Elizabeth stood.

Vianna raised a brow. Her duvet? A bedroom display. The brothel ghosts pressed in, closing in around the circle. That was what they'd done last time. Right before Elizabeth attacked Liam.

Dee twirled her hands in the air. "Let it be done." She looked at Vianna with a cringe. It was all so absurd and they were terrified, but it was something.

"She wants the duvet. Right *now*, James! We have to get the duvet upstairs in the museum!" Vianna grabbed the candle and pushed Dee and James toward the stairs, praying the gun in James's hand didn't go off.

"Hurry, Vie," Tuck shouted from their prison.

The three of them stumbled over each other as Vianna rushed them up the stairs. Both she and Dee pressed James ahead of them, and all three burst through the door. They stumbled into a dark, dusty room, and Vianna felt her hip bump into something hard. The something hard swayed from their collision, and a series of loud clanks clattered against the tiled floor.

"Shit, Vie, there's security in here! They're gonna hear us now!" James turned to run back through the door, but light flooded from the doorway on the other side of the room.

A man with a buzz cut and swollen muscles stuffed into a polo shirt stared at them. She knew that polo shirt. Museum security. The man even had the wired cord in his ear.

"You can't be in here." The security guard pressed a finger to the plastic in his ear. "Break-in at the west storage room."

22

The Magical Duvet

"You need to send someone into the tunnels," Vianna blurted with her hands up, one still gripping the candle, to show she wasn't a threat. "Someone has been hurt badly, shot."

The security guard didn't flinch the slightest at her words, his expression fixed and flat. He swept a muscled arm behind all three of them, propelling them between two metal shelving units and toward the museum. "This way."

"You have to listen to us." Dee yanked her elbow out, trying to break free of their forward motion, but the security guard just shoved harder. "She's going to die. Call an ambulance!"

Once they were in the hallway, James squirmed out of the security guard's grip and darted down the hall. His gun was gone—he must have dropped it somewhere in the commotion. "The duvet," he yelled over his shoulder as he ran. "This way."

The security guard lost interest in Vianna and Dee, chasing after James down the red-carpeted hallway instead. Vianna frantically

198

patted down her jeans for her phone but she'd left it in her backpack. Her heart dropped. "Dee, your phone."

Dee's face fell. "It's downstairs."

Vianna twirled, looking down the other stretch of hall with roped-off display cases and antique furniture, but no actual people. "Where is everybody?" she growled. "The security officer. He has a radio. Come on."

They chased the security guard who chased James around a corner. James pivoted, bunching up the carpet runner as he veered into a display room. Vianna followed just as the security guard tackled James, and they flew into a delicate nightstand beside a large poster bed with a draped canopy. The lamp on the nightstand flung against the wall and porcelain shards shattered everywhere.

"My shoulder," James wailed.

More polo-shirt security guards poured into the room, swarming a shrieking James. Vianna let out a sigh of relief at finding more people; surely someone could help Ashley now. And then Charles rounded the corner in a crisp tux with even more guards flanking him. Her heart sank. He stopped in front of her, glancing behind her to James, wrestling at least four security guards over the damn duvet he'd managed to pull from the bed.

"Vianna? Of course it's you." Charles motioned with two fingers toward James, and several guards went to help their comrades. "Same old Vianna, ruining everything she touches."

"There's a woman trapped in your vault below the museum. She's been shot." Vianna's breathing was ragged. "In the tunnels. She's bleeding out. You have to call an ambulance."

Charles's jaw flexed, and he didn't move a muscle.

"I don't think a dead body is the type of media you want during your campaign." Dee spoke from behind Vianna.

Charles's upper lip twitched, and he turned his back to them to address the closest polo shirt. "Send a team to the vault and take a medkit. Call for an ambulance only if absolutely necessary."

"It's necessary." Vianna spoke through clenched teeth.

"We'll see." He brushed past her, approaching James who had been subdued, pinned flat on his stomach and still clinging to the duvet. "This display is worth millions. Who is going to pay for this?"

An icy chill trickled across Vianna's arms. She clenched her fists against the cold, slowly turning in a circle, looking for any ghosts. The yellow light from the petite chandelier above them flickered. The guards didn't react, focused on James.

"Vie," Dee whispered, also turning in a slow circle.

"Yeah," Vianna said. "I feel it. But I don't see her yet."

"This area is off-limits," Charles barked. "All of you need to leave. And I'll be pressing charges. Breaking and entering. Destruction of property."

"Charles?" Tiphonie's voice came from the hallway.

The temperature in the room plunged further, and everyone's breath came out in puffs. More people, familiar witches in elegant ball gowns, gathered in the hallway. The guards finally realized something was wrong, looking around confused as their breath came out in icy clouds.

"It's all under control." Charles raised his hands to the witches, herding them back the way they came. "Just an attention seeker. She'll be dealt with."

The guards and James paused in their tug-of-war over the duvet. He'd tucked himself into a ball in the corner, mumbling about his show and how they didn't understand. The guards dragged James by his kicking legs into the hallway, with the duvet trailing behind him.

Elizabeth still wasn't visible. Vianna rotated, looking along the length of the bed, the turned-over nightstand, the vanity and mirror, the painting of Elizabeth on the wall—that flickered with movement.

Vianna straightened, slowly shifting back toward the painting of Elizabeth in a princess-cut dress, pink heart lips, and a frizzy updo. The shadows in the painting shifted. The woman's brown eyes darkened to a deep black, and her porcelain skin drooped from her bones, leaving a ghostly skull that lifted from the painting mid-scream. The ghost of Elizabeth stepped from her own painting.

Frost speckled across the mirror on the vanity. Vianna was mesmerized as the ghost of Elizabeth drifted closer. Her lips twisted into a snarl, eyes locked on Vianna. Brothel ghosts floated into the room, filing behind Elizabeth.

"Vianna!" Charles stormed back into the room. "I don't know what kind of spell you put on this room, but this is enough. These pathetic tactics won't work. You missed your chance."

The ghost of Elizabeth hovered closer, ignoring everything in the room but Vianna. The wind whipped hair into her eyes, and she tried to back away, bumping into Charles.

He grabbed her by the arm and jerked her to the side. "Make this stop."

"Don't touch her." Dee smashed her clenched fist into his broad nose.

Charles flew backward, landing flat on his back and splintering the tipped-over nightstand into dozens of wood shards that scattered across the floor.

"Charles!" Tiphonie screamed from the hallway. In a slow pivot, she turned and charged toward Dee.

Vianna spun to intercept, but an ice shard sliced through her chest, freezing all movement. She gasped. Turning her head forward, she saw Elizabeth's outstretched arm extended into her chest. A layer of ice spread through her insides, hardening her organs into frozen chunks. Her breathing came in gasps. The pressure in her chest tightened, and Vianna slid to her knees. The candle she'd been holding plopped against the carpet.

Everything blurred together: Charles wailing about his nose, James's screeching, crashing thuds as Dee wrestled Tiphonie off her, and shouting voices Vianna didn't recognize. The edges of her vision went blurry. She was dying, and there was nothing she could do to stop it. She hiccuped another breath. All movement slowed.

"Shuck," Vianna whispered. A tear slid from the corner of her eye, trailing down her cheek. "Please."

She'd done so much wrong. She'd shut down so many connections that mattered, so many connections that could help her, that could strengthen her, and she'd hidden away. She might have stopped physically running away, but she was doing it mentally. And she wasn't strong enough on her own. She'd done everything wrong.

The marking on her collarbone warmed, and the warmth spread down her chest and over her shoulder as the center turned to a burning heat that she welcomed. A low grumble shook her bone marrow, and instead of cringing or clamping down on the magic, she took a breath and accepted the surge of power.

The ice grip within her chest released, and she opened her eyes. Elizabeth slumped to her knees. Her clawed hand was red as though burned by fire. Her roar shook the poster bed. She rose and snatched the chair from the vanity, swinging it against the bedpost, where it ricocheted into Charles. He yelped and melted into a corner.

"Vie," Dee yelled from the doorway. A gawking crowd had formed behind her. "What do you need?"

Vianna pushed to her feet and flinched against the pain that sliced through her chest. "My backpack. The jar from Tuck!"

Dee bolted. The energy around Vianna was sucked from the room like a mental vacuum on high. Elizabeth pulled from the essence of the brothel ghosts and roared with renewed power. She ripped the painting from the wall and flung it in Vianna's direction.

Vianna swatted at the projectile, sending it into the wall, and a slice burned down her forearm. Elizabeth bared her teeth. Shuck rumbled back in Vianna's chest. She could feel his eagerness to kill, but she didn't pull away from him. With a deep breath, she pushed down the fear that was holding her back and kept her connection to Shuck open.

Elizabeth inhaled the brothel ghosts, pulling their energy. Time was running out. Vianna looked around at her feet for the candle, not seeing it. Wood splinters and porcelain shatters were a plenty, but not candles. She kicked at the debris and lifted the cushioned chair to a vanity that only had two legs left. The candle rolled against her foot, and Vianna snatched it up.

Opening all of herself to Shuck, she focused on the candle, still wrapped with the delicate chain. It needed to be destroyed. A strength filled her as she gripped the candle. It was a burning, growing determination that felt like rage. Shuck released a wet, deep growl. Elizabeth stopped her consumption of the brothel girls, and hazy white tendrils slid down her front side. The brothel girls slid into sprawled, exhausted lumps.

Shuck's growl sounded again, closer this time, stalking its prey. Shadows darted through the room, charging Elizabeth as she lashed at them with her clawed hands. A large dark shadow in the shape of a snout with teeth dove at her, latching onto her arm. Elizabeth's jaw dropped as she roared back.

"Vie." Dee slid to a stop as she careened into the room. She tossed the spell in a jar and Vianna caught it.

Without hesitating, she shook the jar, then popped the lid open. With the connection to Shuck opened and thriving, magic bounced through her body like electrical zaps. She poured the dirt over the candle. "Time to go home."

She chucked the candle with every ounce of strength at the mirror of the vanity. Glass shattered, and a force exploded out from the impact, sending everyone flying off their feet. Vianna used her arms as a shield as a cyclone of wind and broken shards swept through the room and then puffed to a stop.

Silence. The wind stopped. Vianna dropped her hands. The frost had faded. There were no more ghosts, Elizabeth or the brothel girls. But the warmth of Shuck remained. Vianna pressed a hand to her collarbone and let out a deep breath. *Thank you.*

A whimper came from the corner, and Vianna turned to see Charles curled in a ball by the bed. She looked around the rest of the room. Tiphonie and Dee were on the floor a few feet away with disheveled hair and clothes. The crowd of witches in ball gowns were also pushing themselves up from the ground in the hallway.

"She's at peace now?" James whimpered. "With her duvet?" He was slumped in the doorframe, cuffed wrists hanging between his knees.

"No, James." Vianna sighed and walked over to him. She didn't know what peace was like or how it was found for the dead. "Ghosts don't normally care about duvets or telling you their secrets. And they certainly don't care about making you famous."

His face slacked in what looked like regret. "I didn't get any of it on film. What a waste." He pouted. "It's okay. We'll have more backups next time. We know what we're doing now."

Vianna stared at him, anger simmering. He didn't get it. He would never get it. She couldn't find words because there were none that would reach him. Tiphonie rushed toward Charles in the corner. Men in uniforms—real uniforms and not polo shirts—bustled farther down the hallway.

Dee approached. "Cops are here. Grayson helped me get your bag."

Finally something had gone right. "Let's go check on Ashley."

"You are not a spokesperson for the museum." Charles swatted Tiphonie away from cleaning the blood off his nose. He struggled to get up with all the debris. "*I* will speak to the cops. No need for you to spread more lies."

He turned to leave, and Tiphonie followed.

"Stay here," Charles commanded. He straightened his sleeves by pulling on the cuffs.

"Charles," Tiphonie whispered loudly. "I'm a legacy. It's a better image with me at your side."

"I agree with Charles." Zosia Ramsey rounded the corner, her twin daughters at her heels. All three of them wore deep red gowns that matched their lips. "There are plenty of legacies running around to remind the police who rules the roost. You're not needed."

Zosia snapped at a lingering crowd of younger witches in glittery dresses. "Mind your posts." She motioned at her daughters, who bustled off, not even acknowledging Tiphonie.

Charles gave a triumphant smile, patting Tiphonie's hand. "Stay put." He straightened his jacket again and walked away.

Staying with Tiph and a detained James wasn't a priority. Vianna and Dee headed out of the exhibit room and down the hall, toward the bustle of activity pouring from the storage closet with the door to the tunnels.

"Vie, Dee." Grayson raised a hand for them to spot him as he stepped from the crowd, and they rushed to meet him. His expression said nothing, per usual. Trying to read him was pointless.

"How is Ashley?" Vianna blurted. "We sent help as soon as we could."

"They better have made it in time." Dee strained her neck, looking beyond Grayson.

"She's alive. With James distracted and out of the tunnels," Grayson said. "I was able to pick the lock and call for the medics. They just took her. Tuck went with them."

"So why the deep frown?" Vianna asked.

"She wasn't conscious. Breathing, but we'll see if there's any permanent damage when she wakes up. A lot can happen after gun-shot wounds." He rubbed his face with both palms. "I've got a few more things I need to do, but I can have a squad car give you guys a ride to Dee's Jeep."

Vianna nodded. "Okay. Thanks."

"I'll hurry." He turned and joined the other uniforms.

James groaned, still slumped in the doorframe. This was his fault. His delusional ideals of ghosts and demons were just enough to cause trouble. And now he understood that witches were more than the world realized. That was a problem.

"Come on." Vianna tugged Dee's arm. "There's one more thing to handle."

23

The Power of Three

"Whatever your plans are," Dee said. "I'm in."

They marched down the red carpet that stretched over the hallway and stopped in front of James's slumped form.

"Seriously though. What's the plan?" Dee scrunched her face.

Vianna grabbed him by the arm, pulling him to his feet. He whimpered but didn't resist. She shoved him down the hall in the opposite direction of the uniforms, not exactly sure of where they were going. Magic tingles danced in her fingertips.

She turned and pointed to Tiphonie, who stood alone in the hallway. "You too. You're coming with us."

Tiphonie straightened with a scowl. "I'm not going anywhere with *you*."

Vianna paused. "No? Decided being a *trophy witch* for Charles is your path? Your call."

Tiphonie pursed her lips but didn't budge.

"Not making a choice is a choice, Tiph." Vianna shrugged and continued forward, nudging James along.

"Fine." Tiphonie trotted after them. "But I'm only coming to help clean this up for Charles and the museum. Not the two of you."

Tiphonie smoothed out her hair as she trotted beside Dee. Vianna considered their options, passing on the pirate exhibit and instead shuffling them into a smaller room with a locomotive display. It was undergoing some remodeling, with drapes over half of the train parts and piles of tools stacked in the corner.

She shoved James down onto an old train cart with an open back.

"Ouch," he whined. His handcuffs clanked as he shifted around. "You're kinda freaking me out. Why are we in here? We need to get out of the museum. The cops never understand the ghost thing. They're not believers."

Vianna ignored him. "He needs to be bound." She didn't try to ease into her plans with Dee and Tiph. There was no time. Besides, she wasn't exactly the best at warming into things.

"Bound?" James squeaked, shuffling to stand.

Vianna speared him with a scowl. "Dee, do you have something to knock him out?"

"That's easy." Dee fiddled with some bottles in her potion satchel.

"Oh, this is ridiculous. Death is the appropriate punishment." Tiph rolled her eyes.

James jumped from the train cart, but Dee wrapped a hand around his face, pressing a cloth against his nose and mouth. He tried to shove her off, but the fumes worked faster. His movement slowed, his cuffed hands went limp. He swayed, and before collapsing into a heap, he mumbled, "He'll come for me."

"That got weird," Dee said.

Shuck rumbled in Vianna's chest. "No killing," she said, for Tiph just as much as Shuck. "We'll bind him so that he can't cause harm."

"Him?" Tiphonie scoffed. "What could he possibly do that could threaten me? I couldn't care less. Besides, binding someone isn't something a solitary witch can do. You need a coven."

"Technically, coven spells take three witches," Vianna said. "Not three coven-bound witches. Just three witches of any variety as long as one is demon-bound."

Dee was silent, eyes wide. She was never silent, and Vianna winked at her. "Let's do a little magic." This day had been awful, but maybe something good could come from it.

Tiphonie folded her arms with her tiny nose wrinkled.

"Tiph, he knows about legacy witches," Vianna said. "Knows the oldest neighborhood, can point out known witches, and has stolen a spelled candle and understands how it works. He'll figure out more. He'll keep coming back."

Vianna wouldn't kill him, and she wouldn't take his hands like Mother would have, but she would silence him. Tiphonie's brow furrowed, but Vianna didn't push further, giving her a moment to decide. With lips pinched tight, Tiphonie nodded her head in agreement.

Dee wrapped Tiphonie in a giant hug and squeezed. Vianna almost teared up, but she blinked them away.

"All right," Tiphonie said. "Get off."

Dee pulled back with a smile and Tiphonie scowled, but the corner of her mouth twitched into an almost grin.

"Gather around." Vianna motioned to both of them.

Dee pulled a boline blade from her satchel, handing it over to Vianna with a shaking hand. She was nervous. Vianna squeezed her arm in a show of support. There would be no questioning if Dee was truly a witch after this.

With a shimmy of her shoulders, Vianna took a deep breath and focused on Shuck. His reply was strong and deep as he warmed the connection between them, and the promise of magic danced beneath her skin.

Vianna sliced a cut on her palm, then leaned down to James, gripping his neck. "There is power in knowledge. Power is earned, and you, James Hughes, have stolen something not earned." Her bloodied hand tingled with fire. "For that, I bind thee."

Dee was next. Her chest rose and fell and her eyes glistened, making Vianna wonder if she might cry. She wouldn't blame her. This moment was something Dee had wanted for so long. In a smooth, confident movement, she sliced her palm, then repeated the same words Vianna had spoken. The tingle in Vianna's hand spread up her arm.

Dee handed the blade to Tiphonie, who repeated the same ceremonial words and actions. Normally, after the blood of three legacy lines marked someone, they would tie a red ribbon around the neck. Vianna looked around. Duct tape was close enough. She ripped a strip and wrapped it around his neck, then held out her hands for both Dee and Tiph.

"A legacy times three, we bind thee, James, from ever using the craft. By the power of three, we bind words of legacy knowledge from escaping thy throat. By the power of three, we bind thee from speaking of the supernatural."

Tiphonie scrunched her face at the last part but didn't drop her hands. The connection to Shuck swirled like a fire, rising and growing. Vianna dropped their hands and reached for the duct tape, pulling a section of it from his skin. Using the boline stained in blood, she sliced the tape to represent cutting the ribbon. A pop snapped in the air, which exploded with the aroma of roasted marshmallows and anise.

"Tiphonie," roared Charles. He stood at the doorway, veins bulging in his neck. "What are you doing with *them*? You went against my instructions? For *them*?"

His face was beet red. He was in full-on tantrum mode.

"Darling," Tiphonie said, rushing toward him. "It was some cleanup to help you. I wasn't going against you."

"I have the most important campaign in my life at stake. I need a wife I can trust. Who will do what I say. We'll discuss this with Zosia." He stormed away. Tiphonie followed after him.

"It worked." Dee's voice shook.

Vianna smiled at her. "Of course it worked." She rushed at her, wrapping her in a hug.

Dee squeezed back, and they held on to the embrace for a long minute. When they pulled back, Dee grabbed alcohol swabs from her satchel and handed one to Vianna.

With a sigh, Vianna looked down at James. She pressed the swab against the cut on her hand. "How long until he wakes up?"

"An hour at most," Dee said. "I'm sure there will still be cops mingling around. They can deal with him."

"Agreed," Vianna said. "Let's go find Grayson and go home."

2 4

A Mabon Feast

Two Days Later

The change of seasons always created a magic-like beauty in the garden, but there was always something extra special about the final evening of the autumn equinox. Vianna cradled a steaming mug of Mabon cider, the warmth seeping into her palms as she enjoyed a moment of solitude before the chaos.

Along the far end of the yard, creeper vines in brilliant fire tones climbed the wrought iron fence, tangling with the velvet leaves of the berry bushes in the east corner. The rich colors created a warmth that contrasted the nip of crisp air, turning her nose red. She sipped her mug with a grin.

After being able to cast "full-on, real magic"—as Dee called it—she'd been a bouncy ball of excitement for two straight days. She'd truly outdone herself with the Mabon preparations. Large maple leaves floated into the yard from Ophelia's trees, then tumbled onto the ornate oak table set up in the middle of the yard. A cornucopia filled of squash, pine cones, dried oranges, cinnamon sticks, and various herbs spilled across the table, with candles staged throughout.

Stepping over a patch of Cinderella pumpkins, Vianna headed inside through the back door, then froze. The war zone had somehow doubled in the whole thirty minutes she'd been outside. Pie pans, bags of flour, strands of herbs, and teetering stacks of casserole dishes filled every surface.

Vianna took a deep breath. "There's no possible way we can eat all of this."

Dee used her forearm to push an errant curl back into her sunflower bandanna. Sticks of cranberries sprouted from her bun. "I think what you meant to say was thank you bestie—who is both brilliant and gorgeous—for making the most elaborate and perfect feast known to mankind."

Vianna sucked in her lips and nodded. "Took the words right out of my mouth."

A buzzer went off, and Dee turned to pull a round dish of sourdough bread from the oven. Shuck rumbled within Vianna's chest, announcing someone at the door. Since Dee was busy making dinner for the entire population of Salem, Vianna made herself useful by answering the door.

Mistress Layton beamed a smile. She wore a brown-and-burgundy flowy dress and held a covered souffle dish in her hands. But she wasn't alone. Vianna was was certain her jaw had dropped to the porch. Tiphonie stared down at her feet.

Mistress Layton raised her chin. "Mabon is a time to give thanks, and you, Vianna Roots, are blessed with a home full of friends and tradition. Those blessed should care for those less fortunate."

Vianna wrinkled her nose. She *was* blessed. But, since when did Tiphonie fall into the less fortunate category?

The old matron continued. "Charles filed a petition of grievance against the coven over what happened at the museum. He's seeking an alignment elsewhere. Mabon feast was moved from the Parker residence to the Ramsey residence with limited invitation."

The coven had dis-invited Tiphonie to the Mabon celebration, which meant her coven status was being challenged. Charles knew his actions would hurt her. Pulling funds from the coven would be a monumental blow, and all because Tiph had disobeyed him and sided with Vianna. One of these days that dickhead was going to meet up with karma.

Tiphonie picked at her cuticles. "You owe me for doing the binding."

There went the minuscule spark of sympathy Vianna might have had. Charles being an asshole was not Vianna's fault.

"That was your choice." Vianna folded her arms. "I don't *owe* you anything."

"I have nowhere else to go." Tiph's voice was barely a whisper, and she didn't look up.

Vianna twisted her lips to the side. Tiphonie was a pain in the ass and just flat-out mean, but she also seemed lost without her usual entourage, like she didn't fit in anywhere. Vianna understood that all too well. Against her better judgment, she stepped back from the door to give them space to enter her home. "Careful with the cider. Dee's drinks are strong enough to knock even the goddess on her ass."

"Come on, dear." Mistress Layton patted Tiph's back and led her inside.

A tiny blue car stopped in front of the house, and Tuck got out. He jogged up the walkway, and Vianna met him on the porch with a hug.

"Who was that?" She nodded at the blue car that drove off.

"Uber ride." Tuck took a hit from his vape pen. Dark circles tugged on the skin below his eyes. "Just came from the hospital."

"How's Ashley? Any improvement?"

Tuck shook his head. "Still no movement in her legs. Doctors keep talking about how it may not be permanent and physical therapy might help, but she's not ready to listen to anybody. Still won't even talk to me."

"I'm sorry." Vianna sat on the porch swing, and Tuck joined her.

"It's not your fault. Or mine. Ashley made her own choices." Tuck took another hit from his vape. "Ruby stopped by, though. Liam woke up and he's going to make a full recovery."

"If you're interested in learning more about ghosts, I can help," Tuck said. "On the DL, of course."

"Really?" Vianna sat up in surprise. "I'm definitely interested."

Grandma Susannah appeared by the side of the swing. "He is a waste of your time. He knows nothing of witches, living or dead."

Vianna wasn't sure about that. There was more to ghosts than just witch or non-witch, and it was past time she started to learn.

"Good," Tuck said. "I'll keep an eye out for any clients who you could learn from and who would be willing to let a witch come around."

Dee poked her head out from the front door. "Don't think you two can hide away so you don't have to help. Tuck, I need help moving the cauldron. Vie, you're on fire duty. All the candles."

A shiny blue Chevy pulled up to the house and parked. Grayson stepped out and headed toward the house. Grandma growled and vanished.

"Move a cauldron?" Tuck got up from the swing, following Dee back into the house. "Only with witches."

Grayson walked up the porch steps, and Vianna stood from the swing. He held out a casserole dish in offering, and she took it, raising the dish to look at the bottom for clues of what was inside.

"Mama's famous mac and cheese." He waggled his eyebrows as if he'd said something scandalous, and she chuckled.

"So," he continued as he pulled off his glasses and looped them in his shirt. "What does a Mabon feast with witches include? There won't be any sacrifices, will there? Naked dancing under the moon?"

"Only if Ophelia and Mistress Layton get into the backup cider." She bit back a smile.

They stood in the open doorway of the house, the casserole dish between them.

"Have you made a decision?" He looked down at her, brown eyes all intent, and that fresh linen scent spreading.

"Decision?" she asked.

"The informant gig. You willing to make this a more regular thing?"

Why that made her cheeks flush, she had no idea. Well, maybe she did know why. But he was a cop and she was a witch. "I suppose it wasn't all that bad. Working with a cop."

His eyes dropped to her lips. "You're not too bad either—for a witch."

There was some witty comeback she could say, surely, but she was too distracted by his closeness to think. He leaned in closer and her heart raced. Was he going to kiss her? Did she want him to? So much yes.

Someone cleared their throat from the bottom of the porch steps, and Vianna jumped, almost dropping the casserole. Grayson straightened and stepped back.

Ophelia smiled broadly. "Hello, dear. I brought apple chips and cornbread as promised." She held two wooden bowls, one in each arm. "And this must be your officer friend."

Vianna took a deep breath, switching gears and shaking off whatever that moment was. "Ophelia, this is Grayson. He works with the Salem PD." She looked at Grayson. "Ophelia is my neighbor."

Grayson crossed the porch and held out his hand. "Let me help you with those."

Ophelia gladly handed over a bowl and sauntered up the porch steps. The three of them headed into the house, and Vianna led them into the kitchen, stopping with a frown. "There is nowhere to put these."

"Out here," Dee called from the back porch.

Vianna used her hip to nudge open the screen door, holding it for both Grayson and Ophelia to walk through.

"Wow," Grayson said when they stepped outside. "You guys don't mess around when it comes to Mabon."

"Yeah," Vianna agreed. "I'm a little scared for the winter solstice."

"It looks beautiful, dears." Ophelia moseyed over to Mistress Layton and Tiphonie, who were mingling around the table, steaming mugs in their hands.

Tuck and Dee fidgeted with a hanging cauldron that sat on the porch.

"Next time," Tuck said. "We move it *after* you've filled it."

Dee answered by filling a mug and pushing it in his hands.

Everyone helped by bringing the numerous dishes from the kitchen to the table. Dee had place settings laid out and made sure each person had a fresh mug of cider. She directed them all to fill out their hopes or goals for the upcoming season on scraps of paper that were stuffed into the cornucopia on the table. When the guests were settled, Dee picked up the cornucopia and Vianna followed her to the fire pit beside the cauldron.

After Dee placed the cornucopia into the heart of the pit, Vianna reached for the connection to Shuck. Instead of dread, she felt comfort at the warm tingle that answered. When she snapped her fingers, flames jumped to life, both within the fire pit and every candle on the table.

Dee turned to their guests and raised her glass. "We're honored to have friends and family with us for Mabon. May your harvest sustain you and your friendships strengthen you."

A harvest wasn't just for collecting food, but for collecting people. Relationships and people you could trust and experience life with, that was a harvest worth working for. Vianna raised her glass with the others. "Hear, hear."

Everyone clinked mugs and drank to the toast.

Vianna and Dee joined at the table, taking their seats at opposite heads of the table.

"Frankie sent word for you, Vianna." Ophelia was all smiles as she stabbed a slice of ham to put on her plate. "She wanted you to know she'll be docking in two full moons and that you'll be seeing her."

Vianna flinched. More stolen goods from the *Diamond* had appeared around the house: fish nets, coiled ropes, more buckets with various fish, and most recently a giant steering wheel. She was really hoping that was the backup. "Perfect. I think she has something of mine." Hopefully, they could trade goods and call it good, although Vianna doubted it.

Everyone carried on in their own conversations. Tiphonie peppered Ophelia with questions about the upcoming cutting tournament the Lunar Coven hosted every third year. Tuck listened in on their conversation as he stretched out in his chair with his vape. Grayson sat next to Vianna, insisting she load up on mac and cheese, which was probably the best she'd ever had. Dee chatted with her mom about some book collection or another.

And it wasn't just the living gathered for the Mabon feast. Both Grandma Susannah and Clarice hovered in the yard, a good distance from Grayson, but watching. Ghost-beetles spread through her flowerbeds and over the freshly buried tulips.

"This is not a proper coven," Grandma Susannah grumbled.

Vianna had to agree with that point. It wasn't a proper coven, but it was a family.

"So, Dee..." Vianna called to her from across the table. "I was thinking."

Dee looked up from her mug with a raised brow.

"How does Coven Sisters sound?"

"Coven Sisters?" Dee asked.

"For our consulting business." Vianna tried to keep a straight face but couldn't stop the wide grin that took over.

Dee bolted from the table and ran over, wrapping Vianna in a hug from behind. "I knew you'd come around! This is going to be the best. We're going to cause so much trouble."

"I thought our partnership was about preventing trouble," Grayson said.

"It's all in your perspective." Dee flicked her hair as she skipped back to her seat.

Vianna shrugged at Grayson. "Too late to back out now."

"No one said anything about backing out. Someone has to keep an eye on you two."

Everyone happily chatted and ate, different covens, different factions, all together. People. Vianna grinned. Her people. She'd stopped running, stopped hiding, and now she had people. It wasn't all that bad.

25

✦

Epilogue

Csada

He wedged his fingers in between two ribs of the dead creature to get a better grip before he gave a sharp jerk. Bone splintered and blood splattered across his face. He stretched his tongue from the corner of his mouth but could only reach a small drip of blood. He hummed with annoyance. Human tongues were meaty stubs and far less convenient.

Candle light flickered across the stiff hairs of the boar stretched over the wooden block table. The electricity in this dwelling had ceased to work some time ago. He wiggled his toes in the pool of blood at his feet, letting it soak into his pores before it cooled. He sliced a strip of flesh from the carcass and flung it to the floor with a slop. The pungent smell of fresh meat and tangy blood spread through the air, and Csada took a deep inhale, then exhaled with a purr that made his toes curl.

Picking up a soft noise, he tilted his ear to the side. Footsteps shuffled outside the door. He didn't stop his dissection, nor did he remove his arms from the animal. "You were not to come back to me. You were to take the witch away from Salem."

"I tried," the human whined as it stepped through the doorless entrance. "The candle worked, but she broke it. She broke everything. And she bound me from doing *everything*. I can't even say the word gh—gh—g—," it sobbed. "I've tried. And tried." The sack of meat stuttered incoherent and irrelevant nonsense.

"I see."

"I can try again. It almost worked. And if you could undo what she did, I'm certain it would work. She'd see me as an equal and then she'd do the show. I can give you a cut, even let you be a produ—"

"Enough." Csada snapped the rib bone in his hand. The human's prattle was incessant.

Tightening his grip on the curved blade in his other hand, he jerked free of the dead animal. He twirled each knub of a finger around in the fleshy warmth of his mouth, cleaning the blood as he considered his options, of which there were none, really. The human was of no more use to him than the boar.

"Come," he commanded.

Whimpering, the human obeyed. Its limbs trembled as he stood beside the butcher block. Bitterness from its body contaminated the air.

Csada pulled the last finger from his mouth, angling a look at the human. It was within arm's reach. "I will release you of her bonding."

The human slumped with relief, and Csada thrust the blade into his gut. The knife sliced through tender flesh like butter, offering no resistance as he pulled upward. A fresh wave of liquid warmth splashed over his feet. The human's eyes widened; its hands flew up, pressing against Csada's chest, before it slid down into a pile on the ground.

Csada wiped the blood from the blade against his leg, then

flipped it to wipe the other side. Elizabeth had been a gift, and the witch ruined it. The careful planning, the time searching for a demon-touched ghost, the symbolism in using something that belonged to the demon's witch—all destroyed. She was nothing and didn't deserve the demon. Csada slammed his blade into the wooden block.

Simmering with anger, he hummed to himself as he shoved the animal carcass over the edge of the table. It landed with a heavy thud against the tile. The great black Shuck was not a prize to be wasted on a human witch, but should be appreciated by someone who understood the trophy he was—the crowning jewel to the ultimate collection.

Csada hefted the human over his shoulder and flopped it onto the table. Flipping the grip on his blade, he widened the cut through the tender belly flesh and thrust his arms inside the carcass.

The baby witch was in the way, but he would handle her. He would complete his collection.

Acknowledgements

The process of releasing book two was riddled with constant pondering over whether the story had marinated long enough. When you publish a first book, there's so much more fretting with painstakingly longer time frames before reaching the finish line. Publishing book two became about honing a routine that could be scheduled. Phew. It was a ride.

Without my writer buddies, I'm sure I would have completely melted into a pile of my own self-doubt. I'm so grateful for the love and support of my writing tribe. Immy, Poppy, Medusa, and Owen, thank you. Seriously, you guys save me more times than I can count.

And of course, I'm so very grateful for my editor, Brandon Goodmurphy, and the patience he had as I figured out how to polish this beast. My proofreading team over at Darling Axe editing was amazing, yet again. And working with Evelyne Paniez for covers is an amazing experience. I can't wait to see what covers she comes up with for the rest of the series.

About the Author

Cass started her writing career as a journalist in college who moonlighted as an actress. Now at home with her two sons and two dogs, she's discovered that fiction novel writing combines her love of the written word with her love of creating compelling characters.

When not staring at a computer screen, she can be found planting bulbs in the garden, her nose in a book, or watching a horror movie with her teenager.

If you are interested in supporting Cass Kay and the Legacy Witches series, please, please, please leave an online review. You can also email her for information on how to join the ARC team.

authorcasskaywrites@gmail.com
www.instagram.com/casskaywrites
www.twitter.com/casskaywrites

www.ingramcontent.com/pod-product-compliance
Lightning Source LLC
Chambersburg PA
CBHW020654010826
48969CB00013B/2018